P9-CCS-802

MISSISSIPPI CHARIOT

BOOKS BY HARRIETTE GILLEM ROBINET

Mississippi Chariot

Children of the Fire

Jay and the Marigold

Ride the Red Cycle

MISSISSIPPI
CHARIOT

HARRIETTE GILLEM ROBINET

A Jean Karl Book

ATHENEUM 1994 NEW YORK

Maxwell Macmillan Canada

Toronto

Maxwell Macmillan International

New York Oxford Singapore Sydney

Atheneum
Macmillan Publishing Company
866 Third Avenue
New York, NY 10022
Maxwell Macmillan Canada, Inc.
1200 Eglinton Avenue East
Suite 200
Don Mills, Ontario M3C 3N1
Macmillan Publishing Company is part of the Maxwell Communication Group of
Companies.
First edition
Printed in the United States of America
10 9 8 7 6 5 4 3 2 1
The text of this book is set in Granjon
Book design by Claire Naylon Vaccaro

Library of Congress Cataloging-in-Publication Data

Robinet, Harriette.
    Mississippi chariot / Harriette Gillem Robinet.—1st ed.
    p. cm.
    "A Jean Karl book."
    Includes bibliographical references.
    Summary: In Mississippi in 1936, twelve-year-old Shortning Bread
Jackson tries to help his falsely convicted father while dealing with the
troubled racial climate in his town.
    ISBN 0–689–31960–6
    [1. Afro-Americans—Fiction. 2. Race relations—Fiction.
3. Mississippi—Fiction.] I. Title.
PZ7.R553Mi 1994
[Fic]—dc20   94-11092

To McLouis Robinet, my first editor, who sacrifices sleep to finish a reading; my good adviser, who warned me that Sleepy Corners had lanes, not roads; and my best friend, who is a treasured husband.

To my writing critique group: Linda Schwab, Esther Hershenhorn, who asked for this book, Phyllis Mandler, Franny Billingsley, and Myra Sanderman. Thanks for being good friends, giving good advice, and providing good food.

And to the courageous writers and librarians of the Black Literary Umbrella.

MISSISSIPPI CHARIOT

O N E

❦

SHORTNING BREAD JACKSON had a serious need
for time. He had never asked for time off from work,
and he had never received a birthday present. So he decided
to ask for both together.

"Mama," he said that Sunday evening, "tomorrow is my
birthday."

He flipped his suspender strap. The one brown strap fit
over a ragged plaid shirt and was clipped to tan pants cut off
at the knees. The other suspender strap hung free in the back
with a broken clip.

His mama, Claudia Jackson, was ironing clothes. Barefoot,
she wore a faded housedress sewn from flour sacks. Her flat-
iron heated on the wood-burning stove. She turned Mrs.
Abigail Middleton's blue-flowered dress to press the white
collar.

"Birthday? Is that so now?" Mama asked, and took a second iron off the stove. She was strong, his mama, large but
not fat, with earth brown skin like her children. That hot
evening her brown skin glistened like still waters.

She spit on her finger and touched the iron to test it. It siz-
zled just right, so she began pressing the starched collar.

A breeze from door to window blew across the one-room
cabin. It stirred the air and rippled a sheet, hung to separate
the eating and sleeping areas. The breeze was hot and

humid, but nonetheless welcome to Shortning. Their share-cropper cabin stood among two dozen like it in a clearing near cotton fields. Tree-trunk stilts raised the cabin to avoid floods, floods that made the earth in the Mississippi Delta rich for growing cotton.

In spite of the stilts, marks on wooden walls beside him showed where the Mississippi River had risen above the doorsill three months ago to flood inside. All winter long there had been a rumor about how high the yearly spring flood would be.

Mr. Tom Turner had said: "The Mississippi ain't gonna flood high this spring." And all the colored folks repeated it. Then the white folks passed word: "The colored folks are saying there won't be much flooding in the spring."

Sometimes rumors were right, and sometimes rumors were wrong. This year Mr. Tom Turner's rumor had been wrong. Shortning thought nobody really knew until it happened.

Folks in Sleepy Corners didn't bother to think for them-selves. Instead they believed in rumors. When it flooded high, Shortning's family patiently climbed on the roof to wait out the waters like Noah's family of Bible times.

Shortning's sister, Peanuts, was ironing next to Mama. As Methodists, they didn't like to work on Sundays. But it would take both of them three days to finish the loads of laundry from Friday's pickup.

Peanuts held her iron up. It was heavy for her, and wavered in the air. She stared at him. "It ain't no May month yet," she said, and frowned.

"Tomorrow the fifth of May, and I'll be twelve years old," he said, and grinned. Peanuts had ten more months before she would be twelve. Between March and May they had both been eleven. They were about the same height—short for their age— but strong from work, and wiry.

"Twelve already?" Mama asked, and she sighed. She sighed and moaned often lately, and he knew why.

"May?" Peanuts repeated. "I guess it is the month of May. When we out of school, it's hard to remember what month it is."

She wore her black hair in neat cornrow braids. The tattered skirt to her red taffeta dress hung to her ankles. Shortning knew she was proud of the whispering dress that she had picked from the church "charity box." Besides having a lace collar, the red dress made a pretty rustling sound when she walked.

Peanuts screwed up her face and glanced at the calendar nailed to the wall. It would not help her. The month was always December there because Mama liked the red Christmas flowers in the picture. Besides, the calendar was for 1934, and this was May 1936.

"And Mama," Shortning Bread said, "I was thinking."

Peanuts set her iron on the stove and put her hands on her sides. Shortning thought she was so skinny she didn't have hips.

"I was thinking." He took a deep breath. "Thinking maybe I could take the day off from chopping cotton." In May they humped up the soil and weeded around the cotton plants. During cotton-planting and cotton-picking times, he was needed in the fields. He wasn't needed as much to chop cotton.

His older brothers—Elias, who was twenty-one, Jude, who was seventeen, and James, who was fifteen—chopped cotton too. All his friends would be in the cotton fields. This would be a day all to himself, because he needed some thinking time.

Mama was quiet for a long time. Shortning looked at her. His mama reminded him of a strong mountain. Of course living in the flat Mississippi River delta, he had never seen a mountain, but he could imagine. After all, he had the high, mounded-dirt levee. And he worried that his mama's strength might break down in suffering like the levee sometimes broke open in floods.

Already she had started moaning and muttering to herself. And sometimes she forgot what she was doing, or forgot that she was talking to him. How much heartache and worry could his mama stand? Now she shook her head and sighed.

Peanut's grin grew wider. She had just stuck out her tongue at her brother, when Mama said, "Yes."

Peanuts slammed her iron on the ironing board.

"Thank you, Mama. Thank you," Shortning Bread said. "I'll make it up, I promise!" He felt sorry for Peanuts.

Mama pointed her finger. "You'll help Mr. O'Malley with milk delivery, won't you?"

"Yes, ma'am," he said. "Then I'll take the day off."

"And please don't get in no trouble," she said almost in a whisper. "Watch your mouth."

He shook his head no. His throat felt tight. The Jacksons were all trying to act invisible. Trying to act so that no one would notice them, and this was why:

Their gentle father, who never stole from anybody, nor lied on anybody, nor hurt anybody, was serving ten years on the Mississippi chain gang for stealing a car. A car he never saw. A car he couldn't have driven if his head were at the barrel end of a shotgun, because he didn't know how to drive!

Mr. John Putnam from Rock Hill County reported his car

stolen. The sheriff found it smashed in a ditch in Sleepy Corners. Shortning Bread's father, Rufus Jackson, was walking home after helping Mr. O'Malley deliver milk that morning, and Sheriff Titus Clark arrested him.

Everybody, even Mr. O'Malley, said that Rufus Jackson could not have stolen the car. However, Sheriff Clark had said: "I caught him right by it. We have to keep the fear in our colored people, keep them in their place. That's why you folks hired me."

The sheriff went as far as to start a rumor: "If I don't stick to my guns on this Rufus Jackson case," he had said, "the colored people of Sleepy Corners will take to crime: talking back, not showing for work, lying, stealing."

The rumor was ridiculous, but none of the white people wanted a colored crime wave, so Shortning Bread's daddy was sent away for ten years of hard labor on the chain gang. Chain gang prisoners were needed to build railroad tracks in Mississippi.

"No trouble, Mama. I'll watch my mouth," Shortning Bread said, and crossed his fingers.

Toad in the mud, he thought! Somebody had to do something about his daddy, and that somebody seemed to be him. His mama was muttering to herself more and more, his scared brothers didn't go to church dances anymore; and Peanuts was working too hard for a little girl. He had to do something. Had to!

T W O

🌱

*T*HAT MONDAY MORNING of his birthday, Shortning woke himself, dressed, and ate from the oatmeal pot. He pulled on his floppy felt hat, and was out on the road as usual by three o'clock. Sometimes the milk truck was early.

He didn't mind waiting because he thought early morning was the best time of day in Mississippi. Moths with eyespots on their wings fooled him into thinking he saw faces in the dark. He thought the air was so clean and so cool and so sweet you could sip it from a tin cup. Honeysuckle flowers waved fragrance in breezes that seemed to sweeten the whole world. And how the stars flashed their teeth smiling in early morning blackness!

Shortning Bread had begun helping Mr. O'Malley deliver milk the morning after his father was arrested. That was two years ago. The Jacksons couldn't afford to lose a good family job. Mr. O'Malley paid twenty-five cents every morning faithfully. It was three hours work, seven days a week.

When he was arrested, Shortning's father was fearful: "How will you make it, Claudia?" he had asked Shortning's mama. "Will Mr. O'Malley let one of the boys take the milk truck job? Will the ladies still give you their laundry? Will the Wilson brothers let the family work on the plantation, or will we lose our sharecropper cabin?"

Claudia had tearfully hugged him, and then they had dragged Rufus off, looking over his shoulder, worrying about his family. But people were kind. They allowed the Jacksons to keep jobs while Rufus was doing time on the chain gang. The family had suffered quietly until just a few weeks ago, when something exploded for Shortning.

It had happened outside O'Brian's hardware store, when he overheard a conversation:

"Mary," one woman said, "did you know John Putnam's son stole his father's car two years ago and smashed it?"

The other woman said, "That's no news. Boy said he did it. Everybody 'round town knows that. Wasn't no paperwork neither."

"No paperwork?"

"No paperwork sentenced Rufus Jackson to the chain gang." She sighed. "Somebody with a little influence could get him out in a snap. Rufus used to wash walls and chop wood for me. Hardworking man. Shame them Jacksons don't have a colored lawyer."

"Ain't no colored lawyers," said the first woman. "Not alive in Mississippi, if they know what's good for them."

That's what Shortning overheard. The words "somebody with a little influence could get him out in a snap" haunted him. He was his daddy's son. What could he do about it?

He hadn't slept well since hearing that, but he was afraid to tell his mama. He was surprised that people around Sleepy Corners were still talking about his daddy. Some white people knew and liked his daddy. Maybe they felt guilty because that sheriff's crazy rumor had stopped justice. Shortning kicked a stone thinking, as he waited in the early morning.

Wouldn't it be wonderful if he could free his daddy? Everyone knew the arrest was wrong. But how could he,

Shortning Bread Jackson, spring his daddy from the chain gang? There had to be a way. Then they could leave Mississippi. The whole family could start life over in Chicago. Wouldn't that be wonderful?

Mr. O'Malley slowed his milk truck by the longleaf pine where Shortning waited every morning. Shortning jumped on and slapped the fender to let Mr. O'Malley know he was there.

Mr. O'Malley slowed down at every house for delivery. Shortning grabbed quart bottles to put by the front doors, then ran to catch up with the creeping truck. He knew who took one quart, who took two quarts.

Shortning shook his head as they drove past a house. Those people, like some others, had stopped getting milk when they were laid off at the tomato farm. The only work around was in growing cotton or in growing tomatoes. Cotton sold overseas; tomatoes sold up north; up north they just weren't buying them.

Their senator Theodore Bilbo was trying to introduce new jobs: factories. Shortning read about it in the newspaper. But people in Mississippi were stubborn about accepting new ideas. Times were hard in 1936; people were talking about when they'd get out of this depression.

Mr. O'Malley finished in daylight near six o'clock, with the sun glowing hot, cicadas and crickets screeching at jokes, and butterflies busy fluttering pretty. Shortning always noticed the butterflies. Cupping his hands, he caught a katydid. The tricky, light green insect sure did imitate a leaf. He let it go and tucked his hat under his arm respectfully, waiting for his pay.

Mr. O'Malley tossed a quarter on River Road and drove off

over it. Shortning trotted over, pocketed his mama's twenty-five cents, and began to whistle "Honeysuckle Rose." His mama said he had an ear for tunes.

He plopped the tan felt hat back on his head. Its pulled-down brim had an edge he liked; it was rippled from rain-water.

The next song he whistled was "Is It True What They Say about Dixie?" That song and "Pennies from Heaven" were songs he heard over the radio in Hopkins's general store.

Whenever he went to the store, Shortning Bread had a long time to listen to the radio, and to read the newspapers sold there. Unless he was toting a box of food for a white lady, a colored child waited until the last white person came and left, and the store was empty, before he was served.

The plantation store nearer their home welcomed share-croppers, but insisted that they buy on credit. Then they never knew how much they spent, and the plantation store was expensive. The Jacksons bought at Hopkins's general store. They didn't want to owe the Wilson brothers, who owned the plantation.

Now, what would he do with his birthday? How would he come up with a way to save his daddy? Time was important. In a couple of weeks the sheriff's daughter, Maybelle Clark, would marry the Rock Hill mayor's son. The sheriff didn't want anything to spoil his daughter's wedding. He didn't want any trouble in the community, and so wouldn't show his ugly side too easily. Right now Sheriff Titus Clark was as vulnerable as a thirsty turtle trapped on its back in a hot lane. But Shortning knew time was short, and he was alone in this business. If anything was going to be done, he had to do it.

Everyone else in his family was afraid. They didn't want

any trouble. He was afraid too—sleeping at night, he wiggled like a wet worm on a dry fishhook—but he had to do something.

From over the levee he heard boys' voices, so he climbed through stiff wildflowers and grass up onto the levee. Once there he lay flat on his stomach, hidden in scratchy weeds, to watch some white boys swimming. They seemed to be having fun.

They were laughing, but was it funny? They were telling a boy, "Fatty, step over here. You're so fat you'll float on down to New Orleans. Float on down to New Orleans." They began chanting it over and over.

"I can't swim," the white-haired boy called. "Is it safe? How do you float? Can you teach me?"

Shortning raised his head. The Mississippi River dropped deep not far from shore at that point.

Suddenly that white-haired boy was choking and sputtering. "Help!" he called, but his laughing friends took off for shore like chickens after crack corn. They ran up the levee and past Shortning without seeing him. The boy went down twice, and Shortning Bread saw terror on his pale-eyed face as he came up kicking. Shortning tossed his hat. He had to do something or that boy might drown.

He leaped up and slid down the levee. At the bottom he ran into the Mississippi. In midstream Shortning rode the deep water like a bicycle, found the boy, and dragged his face up. Shortning's daddy had shown all the Jacksons how to swim and how to tread water.

The boy coughed, gagged, spit up, and then stared at Shortning Bread. Shortning swam, pulling the boy to where they could both stand and walk. By then they were far down the moving river.

Shortning pushed the boy to walk ahead. He was red-faced and bent over coughing, so Shortning wanted to make sure he didn't collapse.

It was a boy they called Hawk Baker. In their small town of Sleepy Corners, everybody knew everybody's family, black or white. Hawk was about Shortning's age, tall and stocky, and the only child of Mr. Charlie Baker, the postmaster.

"Now go on," Shortning said. "Go on home." He wanted the two of them to separate as soon as possible. This encounter could be twisted into trouble for the Jacksons.

"You saved my life," Hawk said. He gasped and repeated, "You saved my life. You!"

"No, sir," said Shortning. "I just helped. Mr. Hawk, you walked out that Mighty Miss by yourself." That was partly true.

"You were the one who saved my life! You! A colored boy saved me and not my friends."

Shortning Bread knew he had to be careful. Mr. Hawk Baker might change his story and say that Shortning Bread was trying to drown him rather than trying to save him. A colored boy's word against a white boy's lie was worth less than spit.

Shortning quickly passed the boy and climbed up the levee. When he glanced back, Hawk was doubled over coughing. Shortning ran back down, thumped Hawk on the back, and raised both of Hawk's arms.

He glanced around for Hawk's friends. Five brilliant blue butterflies visiting pink clover distracted him for a second. Surely Hawk's friends were coming with men to help save him?

Hawk sneezed. "You saved me." His breathing was loud and raspy, but he walked upright as they reached the top of the levee. Shortning stared around and began trotting down the side, angry now. It wasn't right that he should have to be afraid, have to bow down to this white boy who couldn't even swim.

"You got school now, Mr. Hawk," he called. "Go on now."

Shortning couldn't help but remember that white children, at their separate schools, had a full school term. Colored children's school ended early for planting cotton, and started late after picking cotton.

He was also thinking that if Hawk Baker was going to keep saying he saved him, Hawk could at least say thanks. Shortning was beginning to feel cocky. His mama had warned him to stay out of trouble, but should he have let Hawk Baker drown?

"You saved my life," Hawk said again, standing tall now. He no longer coughed, and they were about to go separate ways.

As he left Hawk, Shortning Bread reached out a hand. A colored boy's hand to a white boy!

Hawk stared at him, stared at his brown hand. "We ain't equal. I ain't shaking your hand just because you saved me!"

"A colored boy is good enough to save your life, but not good enough to shake your hand, huh?" Shortning put his hand down as if it had been burned with a branding iron, turned quickly, and walked toward a shady woods full of live oaks and cypress and gum trees.

His suspender strap flipped against his leg. As soon as he was hidden, he climbed a tree and sat, face in hands.

"I'm sorry, Mama," he whispered. "Toad in the mud! My big mouth gonna get us in trouble yet!"

What is wrong with me? he wondered. Twelve years old

that day, and he still didn't have any sense. He wrung out his clothes and dried them on branches in the sun while he rested in the buff on a scratchy tree limb. His mama's twenty-five cents had stuck to his pocket. That was good luck.

When his clothes were damp-dry, he put them on and climbed down. He walked through pungent-smelling weeds to find his hat, caught a walkingstick and let it go. Nature sure was tricky. Walkingstick insects looked just like twigs from a tree.

But it wasn't walkingsticks that interested him now. It was Hawk Baker. What, he, Shortning Bread Jackson, knew about Hawk Baker could hardly fill a thimble. Hawk wasn't mean like some white boys. Usually alone, he seemed shy and quiet. On Sundays he fished with his daddy, and oh yes, he played piano.

You could hear Hawk playing whenever you walked down the dusty lane near the post office. Hawk played mostly long drawn-out music with returning tunes between loud parts and soft parts. But he could play ragtime too.

Shortning Bread figured that Hawk played blues, jazz, and ragtime when his mama and daddy were gone. How Shortning wished he could learn music. He played music on bones and spoons, and he dreamed of one day owning a harmonica. He had seen how music was written with little dots and sticks. Most white children played music for a couple of years, then quit. Hawk Baker kept on learning new music, so he must like it.

Shortning decided to take the direct way home. He walked past Sheriff Clark's small white house, but it wasn't white now. It was painted blue with white trim. That was strange because almost everybody in town had houses painted white.

Shortning whistled "Honeysuckle Rose." He had heard that Miss Maybelle Clark's bridesmaids were going to wear Alice blue gowns.

In the sheriff's yard Shortning saw some white men building a trellis. He stopped and scratched under his hat. No wonder the sheriff had put fresh paint on his house. His daughter wasn't marrying at the Southern Baptist church, she was marrying in her garden under a trellis. And the sheriff's blue house must match the bridesmaid's blue gowns. He would have to tell Peanuts about that.

He walked slowly along River Road, trying to enjoy the freedom of his birthday, and trying to think. He had a whole day to make plans. What a birthday present his daddy's freedom would make!

Now, what could he do to free his daddy?

S HORTNING BREAD JACKSON walked so slow with his thoughts it was late morning when he strolled past Hopkins's general store on River Road. His thoughts flipped back and forth between trying to plan and seeing what was around him. He heard the lonely call of a sparrow to her mate, and noticed an orange butterfly.

His whole family was hurting. And no one knew what horrors his daddy might be suffering. Shortning made fists of his hands, then opened them. They ached.

Outside the general store stood red-haired Mrs. Priscilla Hopkins. Everyone said Mr. Hopkins deserved better in his second wife. It wasn't pleasant buying there, but it was better than owing money at the plantation store.

Mrs. Hopkins's husband's name was Horace, but she called him, "Horse Face," and the amusing thing was that Mr. Hopkins looked like a pale-faced horse. He was tall, with a bald head, a long nose, and dark little eyes. Lately, he stuttered.

Shortning groaned as he passed. How could he free his daddy? What would make people let him go free? He felt like an electric wire in a lightning storm. Inside he was trembling like those wires. He wondered: if he kicked a stone, would sparks fly from his foot?

Mrs. Hopkins was talkative. Anything she overheard was repeated to everyone who came in Hopkins's general store. He saw Mr. Hopkins inside the store and heard his ring of noisy keys.

How could he free his daddy? The sheriff had arrested him. Who did the sheriff have to answer to? Who was Sheriff Titus Clark's boss man? Besides his wife and two daughters, that was.

Well, surely not the judge who visited the circuit courts. Sheriff Clark was arresting officer, jury, and judge all rolled into one, and no one dared challenge him. But, wait, he was afraid of the FBI. No one in Mississippi ever wanted any federal law people to come around. They wanted state's rights to run their own state. Toad in the mud, that was it! The FBI could frighten the sheriff.

Shortning began to whistle. A nervous whistle. This was dangerous thinking. How could a twelve-year-old colored boy get in touch with the FBI? But, did he need to really get in touch with them?

Suppose he started a rumor that an FBI agent was coming to visit the sheriff about Rufus Jackson? Rumors, that's what everyone in Sleepy Corners believed.

His mama wouldn't like this! It might backfire into terrible trouble; yet it might, it just might free his daddy. Shortning felt frantic. There were less than two weeks before Sheriff Titus Clark's daughter's wedding.

They said that Miss Maybelle Clark was having fifteen bridesmaids in Alice blue gowns, the biggest wedding ever in Sleepy Corners. And Maybelle's daddy had painted his house blue to match the gowns. The sheriff would avoid anything that might spoil Maybelle's marriage to the big-shot mayor's son.

Shortning could put the sheriff under pressure. What if the sheriff thought the FBI was investigating Rufus Jackson? What if the sheriff thought the FBI wanted Rufus Jackson free?

It was ridiculous, but around Sleepy Corners the ridiculous happened. Was it any more ridiculous than his gentle upright Christian daddy being put on the chain gang?

First saving Hawk Baker from drowning, then starting a rumor about an FBI agent! As church bells rang twelve times for noon, Shortning Bread shook his head. His birthday was passing, but what a birthday it would be if he came up with a way to free his daddy.

He turned and passed Mrs. Hopkins again. Leaning a hip against her horse trough, she trailed her hands in the cool water. She stared at him intently, as if to keep him from stealing from her store, although she knew he didn't steal. Talkative Mrs. Hopkins was just the person to start his rumor, and today was the day to begin. It might be good luck to do it on his twelfth birthday at high noon.

Shortning mumbled under his breath, but loud enough to be heard, "Sure be glad when that man from FBI come. Gonna talk to Sheriff Titus Clark. Gonna free my daddy." He kept walking, mumbling the same thing again, as if he never saw Mrs. Hopkins at all.

On purpose the only loud words were FBI, sheriff, and daddy. Mrs. Hopkins fell for it. She stiffened and trotted into her store. He could feel her excitement.

On the next lane he passed Mr. Tom Turner and some other colored man loading tomato crates on a truck. Shortning walked over. If what he hoped would happen did happen, there would be trouble, not now maybe, but soon. He wanted to warn them.

At least Mr. Turner still had his job. The company shipped tomatoes north. The men were talking and joking around.

Shortning whispered: "There might be Mississippi chariot soon. Sheriff might be angry when that FBI man come to see him about my daddy."

He began singing parts of the old hymn, "Chariot Coming for to Carry Me Home." This was a code from slavery days to warn of danger. The chariot carried dead folks to a heavenly home.

Mr. Tom Turner said, "That so?" He began humming the hymn.

Shortning knew Mr. Tom would pass the warning and rumor along. He decided to go tell other colored people.

Time and again he whispered, "Mississippi chariot," but always with a comment about the FBI man. Get that rumor started good.

The responsibility to save his daddy made him feel frantic, but important too. He enjoyed feeling important. It was like being admired for dragging a hundred pounds of cotton on his back.

When he walked down the lane again, behind the store, no one seemed to be in the general store. What, he wondered, had Mrs. Hopkins said? Why wasn't she there? Had she gone up the lane to tell the sheriff?

"Oh, Abraham," a lady called from the lane.

She was a Connors from Swiftdale. His nickname was Shortning Bread Jackson, but his real name was Abraham Lincoln Jackson, because Rufus Jackson was grateful for President Lincoln freeing the slaves. His daddy also thought President Franklin Delano Roosevelt was going to do something good for tenant farmers, just as President Abraham Lincoln had done for slaves.

Being called Abraham made him think again of his daddy. He raised a hand to show he heard the lady standing near the store.

His daddy always hoped for the best. His mama said Rufus was a man who saw the glass half full, while she knew it was half empty! She said Shortning's daddy was a dreamer.

Four years ago Rufus Jackson had even vowed to register to vote. He said, "The law says we can. I want my vote to go to Roosevelt." Shortning shuddered thinking about it.

The evening after his daddy tried to register, men in Ku Klux Klan white sheets beat his daddy up and left him for dead on the lane.

Shortning dragged his feet walking.

He recalled how Elias and Jude took his daddy on horseback to doctors in three counties, and none of the doctors would help. The doctors said he must have done something wrong, and no doctor would see him. So Shortning's brothers brought his daddy home, and his mama nursed him. He was unconscious for two weeks; but he woke up, and he was working again in six months.

The lady had called him Abraham; Shortning Bread was proud of the name his daddy gave him. His nickname came from a love of the skillet bread, and a love for the lullaby: "Mammy's little baby love shortnin', shortnin', mammy's little baby love shortnin' bread!" He could play it well on his spoons at home.

"Yes, ma'am," he answered the lady.

"You on an errand for your mama?"

He looked down. "Yes, ma'am." She wouldn't understand him taking a day off on his birthday.

"Come on in here," she said, waving impatiently. "I need somebody to carry a box to my car."

Shortning walked into the store. For a few moments coming in from bright sunlight, he was blind. The store was dark and stuffy hot. When his eyes adjusted to the dim light, he stared at Mr. Hopkins. His wife had left by the back door. Who was she telling Shortning's story to now?

"I came for my two dozen new canning jars," the lady said. "We got peaches coming ripe."

The store smelled of fresh onions, green cabbage, and dust on the canned goods. Dust danced in the spotlight of white sunshine in the doorway.

"Where's Mrs. Hopkins today?" the lady asked.

"Right out back," Mr. Hopkins said. He walked to the storage room and came back. "I think they'll be delivered by three. Could you w-w-wait a bit?"

"Sure, Horace," the lady said. "I got loads of shopping to do." She smiled and opened her fat white purse.

Shortning thought she couldn't do much shopping in Sleepy Corners. They only had two stores, O'Brian's hardware and Hopkins's general, and one restaurant. And that restaurant only opened on weekends.

"Thank you just the same, Abraham." And she handed him a penny. A shiny Lincoln penny. That was nice because he hadn't done anything for her. And one penny plus four bought a loaf of bread; a penny was good money.

At this point Shortning Bread decided to wait and see if Mrs. Priscilla Hopkins came back to gossip with customers. He hung around the store and watched Mr. Hopkins.

Shortning stood in shadows by barrels of pickles, sugar, sauerkraut, and flour stacked inside the door. The sauerkraut smelled good, but Shortning heard scratching inside the barrel. When he opened the lid, a mouse jumped out. Another mouse lay drowned in sauerkraut juice. A brown moth flew past and got caught in a spiderweb. The spider darted for it, but Shortning freed the moth. His hands were covered with moth dust.

Shortning listened and watched.

Mr. Hopkins stuttered: "I—I—I—can't seem t-t-to find green beans."

"There they are, Horace," a lady said, laughing and pointing to the bin. "Where's Mrs. Hopkins today? She usually waits on me." That was true, Shortning thought. Mrs. Priscilla Hopkins had taken over running the store.

Poor Mr. Hopkins. Shortning actually felt sorry for him. He wasn't like this before.

Shortning remembered the first Mrs. Hopkins, who had been as old as Mr. Hopkins, and very fat. Her face had reminded Shortning of a jack-o'-lantern: snaggled teeth, red skin, crooked nose, and loose white hair. She was kindly, slow, and quiet. Once she gave Shortning and his brothers free ice-cream cups. And she never accused them of stealing.

When she dropped dead from a heart attack, no one blamed Mr. Hopkins for marrying a young widow, red-haired and slender. He had been married to her about four years now, Shortning thought. She was not kindly, slow, and quiet, but mean, fast, and loud!

Well, she'll spread my rumor good, Shortning Bread thought. And he thought about how good it would be to have his daddy home. While he daydreamed, Mrs. Hopkins walked in and caught him by the shoulder.

"Boy," she said, "when's that FBI agent coming to see Sheriff Clark?"

Shortning began to tremble. "Maybe I said too much,

ma'am." What was wrong with him? What trouble had his big mouth gotten him into now? He was almost afraid of what he had started, but he had to do something!

"When?" she asked in a shrill voice, and her fingernails bit into his shoulder like tiger teeth.

He couldn't back out now. Let's see, he thought, it was Monday. He would have to work fast. "I think, I think, the man said Wednesday."

Shortning relaxed a little and took a deep breath. Toad in the mud! His plan was working.

He felt dramatic, so he said: "Wednesday at noon by the general store."

He had started to say, high noon. Didn't important things happen at high noon? He had to tell his family about this, carefully, one at a time.

When she let him go, Shortning Bread ran out of the store so fast he met his breath before it left his mouth.

F O U R

🌿

HE NEXT DAY WAS TUESDAY. After Shortning delivered milk with Mr. O'Malley, he went to chopping cotton. In the cotton fields he talked to his brother Jude. "Listen," he said, "I got me a plan to free our daddy."

Jude never missed a stroke with his hoe. Even in the dust Jude managed to stay neat. He was dressed in a short-sleeve shirt and overalls. His girlfriend, Annie Louise, worked nearby.

"Well, watch your step," he said between chops at the cotton row. "And don't tell me about it. That way I won't have to tell Elias."

Their oldest brother, Elias, was as bad as a parent, and with Daddy gone, he was worse. Shortning sighed.

Jude had not said not to try his plan, just not to say what it was. Shortning didn't know whether to be glad or sorry. Maybe he wanted Jude to stop him. But with Mrs. Priscilla Hopkins talking, he couldn't stop now.

Jude said, "You're crazy, but you're smart. I remember when you got fat old Mrs. Hopkins to give each of us a free ice-cream cup." He laughed.

Yes, Shortning did that on a dare from his brothers. He bet old Mrs. Hopkins that Mr. Hopkins wouldn't remember where he laid his keys. And the three boys had won free ice cream. Shortning straightened up and looked around.

"If Daddy gets free, we'll be able to go to Chicago," he said.

Jude tightened his lips and nodded. Shortning realized that Jude was afraid of leaving Annie Lou. He always got tense when they talked about Chicago. But like Daddy, Jude wanted to stay out of debt to the Wilson brothers.

Sharecropping was next to slavery for binding folks to the boss men. By November the cotton had been picked and sold. Then the Wilson brothers had the settle. Folks' cabin rent, store credit, seed cost, and tool repairs were subtracted from pay for working the cotton field all year. The Jacksons didn't buy on credit from the Wilson brothers' store. They worked extra jobs to pay when they bought, and they bought from the general store. They usually came out without debt, but they never could tell. The Wilson brothers kept the books, and they had the last word.

Shortning cleared his throat. "I need time in town," he said. He had started the rumor; now he needed time to work out the details.

"Go," Jude said. "I'll cover your work."

"And someone needs to find the safest routes out of Sleepy Corners."

"I'll tell Elias." Jude stopped and scratched his side. "About a route out, not about your crazy plan. Now, git!"

Shortning dropped his hoe and slipped away.

On the other side of Sleepy Corners that Tuesday morning Shortning Bread met his sister, Peanuts, carrying Mrs. Abigail Middleton's laundry. Washed, starched, ironed, and folded, the laundry was in a bushel basket lined with white oilcloth. Oilcloth covered it too.

Peanuts wore a wide-brim straw hat with daisies perched

on it, and her red taffeta dress. The tattered dress rustled pleasantly as she walked.

"Peanuts," Shortning Bread said breathlessly, "you'll never believe." He skipped along beside her. "Daddy gonna be free soon."

Peanuts looked at him and shook her head no.

"Take this basket like a colored gentleman, Shortning Bread," she said. "My back hurts. Some of us work hard! What are you doing in town today anyway?"

He ignored that. "Listen, listen," he said, skipping beside her. He wiped his face on a damp handkerchief and took the laundry basket. "Peanuts," he said, "Mrs. Priscilla Hopkins is telling folks that an FBI man is coming to talk to Sheriff Clark about our daddy."

"You lying!"

"On my mama's heart, I swear!"

"Who says? How do you know?"

Shortning took a deep breath. Should he tell Peanuts the whole truth? "I just know is all. Sheriff Clark gonna be angry. Mississippi chariot for sure. But Daddy"—he started to say, might be free; he changed it to—"will be free soon." The sound of the words made him feel good.

He felt much better now that Peanuts knew. News of rescuing Hawk Baker from drowning the day before, and news of Maybelle Clark's trellis wedding flickered in his mind, but he didn't want to break the happy mood of news about Daddy. They walked slowly, tasting the delicious thoughts.

Shortning sang:

"I looked over Jordan and what did I see,
Comin' for to carry me home?

A band of angels comin' after me,
Coming for to carry me home.
Oh, swing low, sweet chariot,
Comin' for to carry me home,
Oh, swing low, sweet chariot,
Comin' for to carry me home.
If you get there before I do,
Comin' for to carry me home,
Tell all my friends I'm comin' too,
Comin' for to carry me home, oh . . ."

Generally Shortning would tell things to Peanuts that he couldn't tell anyone else. He would tell her about nightmares he had when some colored man was hung by a lynch mob; nightmares when a colored family's cabin was burned down with them inside.

He could tell Peanuts, but when he told his mother she would repeat the verse of the psalm: "'I sought the Lord and he answered me, from all my terrors he set me free.'" She'd say, "The Lord never lets us down, Shortning."

His father would look at him and say, "Men got to be strong. Things bound to get better one day."

Elias, Jude, and James would shrug and look away. Only Peanuts understood. She would just hold his hand.

Remembering his daddy brought tears to Shortning's eyes. His tall, strong daddy loved to pet chickens. His mama was the practical one who wrung off the chicken's head for Sunday dinner.

And his daddy didn't own a gun. He never hunted possum or coon like other men because he hated to kill an animal. He knew how to heal birds with broken wings. And he could whistle birdcalls well enough to confuse the birds; birds would circle him to stare. Shortning loved to whistle too. He wanted to be as good as his daddy.

But Shortning could wake himself up in the morning. It took all the family to wake his daddy up, and half the family to keep him awake long enough to head out to deliver milk. Shortning smiled thinking about it as he trudged beside Peanuts.

He noticed the clock on the bank read 9:30, 9:30 Tuesday morning. He had to plan how to get an FBI man to Sleepy Corners at noon tomorrow. Wednesday. The thought was thrilling and terrifying at the same time. Their feet raised puffs of dust as they walked side by side down the lane. Was that gardenia fragrance he smelled from a yard?

"Hey, look at that." He pointed to Sheriff Clark's blue house on the other lane.

"I know," Peanuts said. "He painted it blue for Miss Maybelle's garden wedding. See the trellis? But tell me about Daddy. Do Elias, and Jude and James—"

"Jude knows!" said Shortning, hugging the laundry basket. "I warned Mr. Tom Turner and some other folks there might be trouble after." Heat rose from the white dust in waves, and his shirt was clinging to his back, glued by sweat. Cicadas screeched in hot harmony like grease sizzling on the stove.

They reached Mrs. Abigail Middleton's white bungalow. Peanuts opened her squeaky picket gate, and they walked to the servants' entrance at the rear of the house.

Peanuts whispered, "Mama says to try and get her money. Mrs. Middleton ain't paid in two months for her weekly laundry. She owe mama two dollars."

"I got an idea," Shortning Bread said. He grinned and dropped the laundry basket on a broken chair in the backyard. "Go ring the doorbell," he told Peanuts.

Reading glasses perched on her nose, Mrs. Abigail Middleton came to the door. "Well, bring me my clean clothes, Peanuts," she said. She was a barrel-shaped lady with bulging eyes, jet black hair, and skinny legs and arms. She looked like a bug.

Peanuts opened and closed her mouth. She looked at the ground, stony with straggly green grass. She twisted the hem of her skirt. "Please, ma'am," she asked, "Mama say could you please pay me, if you please, Mrs. Middleton?"

"Never mind what your mama say. Just bring me my clothes."

Peanuts dropped her skirt and turned to pick up the basket.

Shortning called loudly, "Sister, is Mrs. Middleton gonna pay her bill?"

Peanuts's eyes sparkled. "No, Brother. She say just bring her the clothes."

Shortning yelled, "Lordy, Mama gonna beat us! Mrs. Middleton ain't paid for her weekly laundry in over two months. Three dollars, ain't it?" And as he acted, he was thinking: We might just need that money right away if Daddy gets free. Need it badly.

Peanuts covered her smile. "Brother, we can't get Mama's money. I gotta do what Mrs. Middleton say! Now let me have her clean clothes."

Shortning heard a neighbor open her back door. He wailed louder. "Oh, no, Sister. We ain't got money for beans unless Mrs. Middleton pay for her clothes." He danced and cried.

He wiped his eyes and howled. He added: "And you know what Mrs. Hopkins is saying at the store."

Peanuts watched, and twisted the hem of her skirt. Finally she ran to hold him. "Don't cry so, Brother," she called.

Another neighbor looked out at the commotion in Mrs. Middleton's backyard. Doors opened across the lane.

Mrs. Middleton ran for her purse. "Here, you pickaninnies," she called. "Bring me my clean clothes!" She threw three dollar bills on the ground. Shortning Bread snatched them up.

Peanuts lifted the clothes and carried them up the back steps. "Thank you, ma'am," she called. "Thank you."

But as Mrs. Middleton closed her screen door, she heard Shortning Bread ask, "Do she know what Mrs. Hopkins is saying?"

Pulling her squeaky door open, Abigail Middleton screeched, "What is Priscilla saying? What is she saying? About me?"

Shortning Bread jerked the empty basket from Peanuts and raced away in the white heat. He raised dust running down the lane. When Peanuts caught up with him, she asked, "Why? Why did you say that?"

"So she can hear from Mrs. Hopkins about that FBI agent. Mrs. Middleton's a big gossip. She'll help spread the word."

When they rounded the corner, Shortning Bread squatted under a crape myrtle bush in lavender bloom. He stared down the lane. Sure enough, Mrs. Abigail Middleton was huffing her skinny-legged way toward Hopkins's general store.

Shortning rubbed his hands together in glee. His plan was working; but a sad thought crossed his mind.

Sheriff Titus Clark probably thought he was just doing his duty. He wasn't mean to white people. At Christmas, Shortning had tiptoed by the white Southern Baptist church window and had seen the sheriff hugging kids as a jolly Santa Claus. The sheriff and Mrs. Clark never had children of their own, but they had raised two girls whose mother had died. Maybelle was one of them.

However, Shortning Bread Jackson had to save his daddy. Sheriff Clark was the man who sent Rufus Jackson to the chain gang. Titus Clark silenced good white people with a rumor about colored folks. Well, one good rumor deserved another. Now to deliver the FBI man!

F I V E

🌾

SHORTNING SWAGGERED AWAY from Peanuts. It was about 10:30 then. The more people who believed his story about the FBI man, the bolder he felt. He almost believed his own tale. Now, how could he get an "FBI-looking person" to arrive at noon on Wednesday at Hopkins's general store?

When he passed the sheriff's house, he saw that the trellis was almost finished. Maybelle, hands on fat hips, stood watching the workmen. A boy was clipping the sheriff's hedge, another boy dug around the sheriff's roses. They were making the yard pretty for Maybelle's wedding.

Shortning slipped down a back-of-town lane and moved quickly down the road out of town. Few cars passed him. Most drivers went to Lewis Lands. That was a big town, he had heard. Sleepy Corners was small.

Finally he came to the corner where two roads parted. He watched people slow down and look at the signs at the corner. One read Lewis Lands, the other read Sleepy Corners. Any cars that came while he watched went to Lewis Lands. Toad in the mud!

Suppose, just suppose, someone changed that sign tomorrow, say at ten minutes to twelve? Then a strange white man might drive into Sleepy Corners. The first place he'd find people to ask where he was would be the general store on

River Road. Unless he asked along the cotton fields, or along the tomato fields.

But, just maybe. Shortning rubbed his hands. The signs swung on a metal pole. Push the sign around and Lewis Land would point to Sleepy Corners. The pole was loose enough. All he needed was just one white stranger.

And Jude was the brother who asked no questions. James was too timid, Elias too responsible. Jude would do it. He hurried off to find Jude, explain what was needed.

When it was nearly noon Tuesday Shortning strutted back into Sleepy Corners and caught up with his sister. She had picked up more laundry for Mama. He was practically dancing in the dust.

"Shortning Bread Jackson," she said. "What're you up to?"

"I tell you an FBI man is coming to talk to Sheriff Clark. And Daddy gonna be free." As he spoke, Shortning realized what a leap there was between someone talking to the sheriff, and the sheriff freeing his daddy. Well, he was doing something. And something was better than nothing. He giggled.

"Hey, boy," called a voice.

Shortning Bread turned to see Hawk Baker beckoning from his father's mail truck.

"Oh, toad in the mud," Shortning Bread mumbled. He had actually forgotten about saving Hawk Baker from drowning the day before. He hadn't even told Peanuts about it. Any other time that would have been big news. But the plans for freeing his daddy had been circling in his mind like a turkey vulture over a dying dog.

Peanuts turned. "What's he got on you? You get in trouble because of that FBI agent? Did you?" she whispered. "Go on."

He swung his hands and walked over to the truck. His loose suspender strap suddenly bothered him. "Yes, sir," he said, eyes properly down on the dirt road.

"You Rufus Jackson's son?" asked Mr. Charlie Baker. He wore a flat-brim straw hat, and his postmaster shirt.

Shortning's back straightened like a broom handle. "Yes, sir," he said loudly. His nostrils flared, and he pressed his lips together. He even briefly glanced into the white man's face. Yes, he was Rufus Jackson's son, and he was proud of it!

"I told you it was him," Hawk Baker said. "I told you, Daddy." He turned to ask, "Don't they call you Shortning something?"

Didn't this white boy ever eat shortning bread? "No," Shortning said, feeling angry and cocky.

Peanuts ran up. "Yes, sir. They call him Shortning Bread, not Shortning Something." She took her brother's hand.

"I told you so, Daddy," Hawk said. "I told you so."

"But his real name is Abraham Lincoln Jackson," Peanuts added with a smile. She swished her red taffeta skirt and glanced down.

Shortning glared at Hawk. The white boy still hadn't said, Thanks for saving my life.

Without a good-bye, Postmaster Charlie Baker started his motor. As the mail truck rolled away, Peanuts pulled her brother's arm. "What does that mean? Tell me!"

"Wait," he said. "I'll tell you all about it."

His floppy felt hat shaded his face and cooled his head in breezes through well-cut holes, but his clothes were stuck to him from perspiration. The month of May was hot in Mississippi.

The loose suspender strap hit his leg in rhythm as he

walked beside his sister. Sometimes that broken strap bothered him, but he wanted to wear those suspenders until he saw his daddy again.

The Christmas before Rufus Jackson went to jail, each of the Jackson children got one Christmas gift. Shortning Bread's present was the brown suspenders. His daddy chose them. He knew that, because they were just like his daddy's.

As they walked, Shortning Bread tried to imagine what might happen when the sheriff talked to a stranger. By now the sheriff knew that an FBI agent was coming. How was he feeling about it? Was he nervous? Angry? Afraid?

The brother and sister reached their favorite hiding tree. Peanuts stored her laundry basket in mossy shade, and they climbed up to talk in secret. Shortning hoped Hawk and his postmaster daddy wouldn't ruin his plans. Why did they need to know who he was?

S I X

❦

*P*EANUTS AND SHORTNING BREAD sat hidden high in a dense live oak by the lane. Like tangled gray-green hair, Spanish moss hung from the tree's branches. As they sat and watched people from their perch, Shortning swung his legs and told Peanuts about saving Hawk Baker the day before.

"But, he ain't my problem now. Now I'm worrying about that FBI man."

"How you know he's coming?" Peanuts asked. "Who told you?"

"Never mind. You believe me, don't you?"

She sighed. "I know lots of white folks feel bad about Daddy. People like our family. That boy even told people he did it. But the sheriff scared the white folks."

Shortning wished he felt stronger. If he could only make some white person feel guilty enough to do something, some white person with influence. As a colored boy he had less influence than a boll weevil.

As he sat and thought, he could hear, not far away, a gang of white boys racing one another home for 12:30 lunch.

"I hear it was some sad," the first boy called out.

"Drowned dead singing, 'Save me, Lord,'" said a second boy.

"Who?" asked a little girl ahead of the boys.

"Hawk Baker. Ain't you heard yet?"

"Drowned in the Mississippi yesterday morning." The boys ran past her.

She stopped to cry. Wailing and sniffing, she trudged home slowly; the untied sash of her yellow dress trailing in dust.

Peanuts elbowed Shortning Bread. They both giggled into their hands. Peanuts almost fell out of the live oak.

Then she pointed. Shuffling behind the next wave of schoolchildren came Mr. Bill Brown. A red-pocked face, bleary blue eyes, and lumpy nose lifted above his short, swollen body. He dressed in cast-off clothes, and sleeping in them added certain wrinkles and odor.

As the county drunk, Mr. Bill Brown accepted food from coloreds and whites alike. He even came to Shortning's mama for a handout, but thirst ruled his life. He lived from drink to drink.

Shortning Bread rubbed his hands. "Just the man. He should know about that FBI agent talking to Sheriff Clark. He should be there Wednesday. The more white people around, the more embarrassing for the sheriff." For a moment he saw the Sheriff as Santa with white wig and beard. His rosy, blue-eyed face made a perfect Santa.

"How you gonna tell Mr. Bill?" Peanuts asked.

"Wait," Shortning said. "I'm thinking."

As children ran below them whispering of the drowning, Peanuts started to climb out of the tree. Shortning caught her red skirt and shook his head no. "But we have to talk to Mr. Bill Brown," she said.

He held a finger to his lips for silence.

As Mr. Bill shuffled near, Shortning said aloud, "You think it'll really be there?"

Peanuts raised her eyebrows and shrugged. "Sure will be, Brother." Her face wore a puzzled grin.

"A hundred-dollar bill?" asked Shortning Bread. "Why you think that stranger gonna dump money Wednesday at high noon?"

Peanuts grinned and said, "Won't he have a bottle of something too, Brother?"

"Toad in the mud, Sister," he said. "He sure will. Gonna hide money and bottles in Hopkins's general store."

Mr. Bill slowed down. He scratched his stubby beard and looked all around. He turned a complete circle looking and listening. He stooped low to stare, but he never looked up. Shaking his head and patting his chest, he stumbled on.

"Where?" Peanuts called.

"General store."

"I bet there's even more than a hundred," she called.

Mr. Bill Brown jolted his squat, swollen body with each step. A few seconds after he passed, his body odor reached the children in the tree. Peanuts waved a hand in front of her face. Shortning Bread pinched his nose shut.

Another crowd of excited kids passed, talking as they skipped along. Above them Shortning tasted the dust they raised.

"Mama say they ain't home," a little girl said. "She called to pay her respects to the Bakers, but they gone."

"At the funeral home," her friend said.

"Bought a fancy metal casket for Hawk," another child

added. "Poor Hawk. First child to drown in the river this year."

"Didn't two colored children from Rock Hill County drown last month?" asked another child.

"They don't count. Like I said, Hawk the first child to drown this year."

When the schoolchildren passed, Peanuts climbed down limb over limb. Shortning dropped from the tree with a thud. It was just like Sleepy Corners, he thought, to pass a rumor that Hawk Baker drowned. Nobody had proof. Nobody had spoken to Hawk's folks. But the rumor was growing by the minute. Just like his rumor about the FBI. It gave him hope.

"You go on home," Shortning said. "I got business."

"Where you think you're going, Shortning Bread Jackson?"

"To see about the government man."

Her eyes grew wide. "Lordy, if I don't believe you! You something else, Shortning. I remember when you talked the electrical pole men into putting a pole down the lane by the cotton fields. They believed you." She giggled. "Ain't nobody hooked up, but we still got an electricity pole on our lane."

Shortning said: "This is serious, Peanuts. When Daddy come home, we'll have to leave for Chicago, you know. Sheriff Clark don't like to be shamed."

Hands in pockets, he strolled away, aware that she stood gazing at him and smiling a few seconds longer before picking up her mama's laundry basket. Shortning grinned. He enjoyed Peanuts's admiration. He was glad he hadn't told her the whole truth.

So kids thought Hawk Baker was drowned. Hawk was

still staying away from his friends, still cutting school. Maybe he wanted them to feel guilty?

Well, that's what Shortning was doing, making folks feel guilty. Mrs. Hopkins had spread with vigor the news of the FBI man. There was so little news in Sleepy Corners. Now maybe she would start telling about Hawk Baker's drowning.

I hope that don't keep people from showing up at the general store at noon tomorrow, Shortning thought. I want them all there, coloreds and whites. Make that sheriff's face turn redder than his neck.

Shortning snorted a laugh. This is crazy, he thought. Hawk Baker ain't drowned, and ain't no FBI agent coming. Lordy, if I ain't believing lies myself.

Suddenly his breath came in gulps, and he felt dizzy. Peanuts believed him. Jude believed in him. Jude was going to turn the sign on Wednesday, then change it back and return to chopping cotton. What would happen? This was such a crazy idea, but sometimes crazy ideas worked. And sometimes they didn't.

Shortning's knees grew weak. He was afraid of mean white people. They had power, power over colored people. Hawk was white. The sheriff was white. Maybe Hawk would grow up to be mean to colored people. Why had he, Shortning, saved a white boy's life? There might have been one less white Mississippian.

Shortning shuddered in the blazing heat because he knew better. He saved Hawk Baker because Hawk was human and needed help. Shortning didn't want to be mean. He didn't want to cave in to anger and hate. He didn't want to lose his mind and mumble to himself, or thrash out at the world. That's why he saved Hawk. His Mt. Olivet minister preached to him; his mama and daddy talked to him; and he figured things out for himself!

All people deserved decent treatment; his daddy deserved decent treatment; and he was going to free his daddy or else!

S E V E N

꧁

TUESDAY AFTERNOON ABOUT four o'clock
Shortning helped Peanuts again. This time she was
delivering butter and eggs for the O'Brians. He had never
realized how hard she worked. She finished in an hour, and
they walked back into town.

Shortning Bread looked over his shoulder because he heard
footsteps thudding on the dusty lane. He moaned. Hawk
Baker was running straight for them. Shortning struck the
empty wooden egg crate with his fist.

"Watch out," called Peanuts. "You'll break it."

"Him!"

She saw Hawk. "Maybe he want to say thanks?"

Puffing his breath, Hawk almost ran into Shortning.
"Hey," he said, "I was looking for you."

"Go away," Peanuts said. She shook a finger in his face.
"You gonna get yourself in trouble, Mr. Hawk Baker. You
ain't supposed to be talking to no colored children."

"Besides," said Shortning Bread, "you supposed to be
drowned dead. All your classmates think so. You didn't go to
school yesterday or today."

Hawk squinted pale gray eyes; his face was red from running. "My friends splashed out of that river, leaving me to
drown." He shook his head slowly. "All of them, all of them
left." His voice trembled, and he pointed at Shortning. "And

4 1

you saved my life, you, a colored boy!" He rubbed his sun-whitened hair.

He said, "I asked if I could go in the river with them for . . . for a special reason. They knew I couldn't swim. William told me to step over to the right. He knew it was deep there." He pointed to Shortning. "You saved me from drowning!"

"Sure," said Shortning. "I'm good enough to save your life, but you couldn't shake my hand." What was he saying? Was he being mean?

"You're colored. Negro. I'm all confused. I don't know much about coloreds. We don't often have them work for us, but I never seen Daddy shake no colored man's hand. Senator Bilbo wouldn't shake no colored man's hand."

Peanuts waved Hawk away. "Go. Get away from here now."

"Wait, listen," Hawk said. "Let me tell you how it is. Kids call me sissy for playing piano. And they say I'm fat. They don't want to play with me. When I walk in the swamplands with them, they get me lost and run away. Then yesterday in the river . . ."

He covered his face with both plump hands, and Shortning Bread wondered if he was crying. He and Peanuts stared at him.

Hawk said, "I wasn't gonna go to school. My daddy said it was all right. That was a special day for me."

Was he really going to cry on them? They were at a bend in the lane. No houses were near, but birds sang in a cypress tree. Hawk was all choked up. He couldn't talk, so Shortning decided to break in.

"It was my special day, not yours," Shortning said, thumb tapping chest. "That's why I wasn't chopping cotton with my brothers on Wilson land. That's why I was there to drag you out of Mighty Miss."

"Well," said Hawk, "yesterday I was twelve. It was my birthday, and I almost drowned on my birthday."

"No, you weren't. I was twelve yesterday."

"You couldn't be," Hawk said, looking at Shortning. "You're too small for twelve. It was my twelfth birthday."

Shortning raised his fist and leaned forward. "I say it was my twelfth birthday. I know when I was born!"

Hawk raised an elbow in defense. "All right, you're twelve." He glanced at Shortning's skinny arms and legs. Shortning Bread lowered his fist and stared back. As they stood, noses an inch apart, a white butterfly fluttered past.

Shortning turned from looking at Hawk and watched the butterfly. He loved butterflies as his father loved birds. He heard some people collected them and pinned them in boxes. He could never pin down a beautiful butterfly; he wanted them to live. He thought moths and butterflies were winged happiness.

Hawk Baker was still staring at Shortning Bread. "Well, do we both have the same birthday? When were you born?"

"May fifth, 1924," Shortning Bread said.

"Me too. Could you and me have the same birthday?"

Peanuts covered her mouth giggling. "It could mean that you're twins," she said, and shook her head, "but I don't think so." She snickered some more.

"So the least you could say is thank you," Shortning said.

Hawk waved his hand. "I'm confused."

"It's not too confusing," said Shortning Bread. "It's just two words, thank you."

"Or just one word, thanks," said Peanuts. "It's pretty painless if you're colored. Maybe it's different if you're white." She slapped her forehead, covered her mouth, and shook her head. She turned sideways, noticed something, and pointed.

A pig was loose and waddled down the lane. Hawk and Shortning looked. "I wonder whose pig that is?" Shortning asked. He stared both ways on the lane.

"Look," Peanuts said.

The pig reached the ditch and leaned over it. Two or three times it tried to reach the water with its snout.

Finally it slid down the side and splashed into the ditch. When it hit the water, it gave a deep squeal.

Shortning Bread, Peanuts, and Hawk giggled in a pile of arms and legs. Hawk bumped his head against Shortning's shoulder, and Peanuts threw her head back in laughter. A few seconds later they all looked at one another. They straightened up.

Peanuts covered her face with both hands. Shortning shook his head. What was he doing? Laughing with a white boy! What were they getting themselves into?

A car motor sounded on the curve. The three kids scrambled to leave before anyone saw them talking. Shortning and Peanuts trotted off together along one bend of the dusty hot lane. Hands in pockets, Hawk followed them.

Peanuts moaned. "It's late. I got to get Mama's laundry and set it to soak, or she'll kill me."

"I'll help you do wash," Shortning said, taking her hand.

"Hey, can I come?" Hawk asked. "I don't even know where you colored people live." The car passed them.

"And you don't need to," Shortning told him. "You just go home, Mr. Hawk."

Hawk stood in glaring hot sun watching their backs and dusty footsteps. Perspiration made his shirt cling to his body like a new sausage skin. "I do so need to know," he called. "Hey, I don't know her name either." He pointed to Peanuts.

Over his shoulder, Shortning called, "You don't need to know my sister's name, white boy!" He began to run with Peanuts.

Hawk stood in the middle of the dusty lane. Hands deep in pockets, he hunched his shoulders. "Hey," he said in a soft voice, "come back here and play." Shortning glanced over his shoulder. Hawk looked lonely standing there.

First, Hawk took shelter under the dense shade of a live oak; then he began following Shortning and Peanuts, running from one patch of shade to another.

Up the lane Shortning and Peanuts saw a crowd of ladies outside Baker's long white cottage. The front room of the house served as the post office. Sunshine blasted fragrance from a garden of red, white, yellow, and pink roses set like a checkerboard beside the house. Shortning pulled Peanuts's arm to take another lane. In passing they heard snippets of conversation:

"First child to drown this year."

"Charlie must be at the funeral parlor."

"Closed the postal service for the day. I went in."

"What a shame. Nice young man like that. Played piano so pretty like. Gonna have a violin quartet at his funeral."

Down the next lane two ladies on a front porch weren't talking about local news of Hawk Baker's drowning. One lady sipped lemonade, clinking ice in the glass. She rocked and sighed. "My husband says they better watch out for that Hitler. Says he's sounding wilder every day over there."

Her friend clinked her ice and said, "Huh! Hitler's harmless. Just putting the fear of God into a few Jews is all. King Edward better watch out for that Mrs. Wallis Simpson."

Head tossed back, her friend cackled like a thirsty hen with fresh water. "She's the one better watch out. He'll never marry that hussy. Why he'd have to leave his throne."

Shortning and Peanuts left the road to pick up the laundry basket, once again stored in a swamp. The wetlands were filled with dense live oaks covered with Spanish moss, and bare-trunked cypresses looking naked among them. Cypress trees lifted feathery crowns to the blue, while lumpy roots crowded around. Black earth squished spongy wet, cooling feet. Leaves smelled good.

Some white boys were tramping in the wetlands. A wood duck flew out to sunny water, began dipping a wing and frantically swimming in circles. It seemed to grow weaker and weaker.

"Look, it's hurt," said Peanuts. "Did those boys hit it?"

Shortning grinned. "Maybe not. Sometimes ducks act injured to lead danger away from their nestling babies. Animals trick people for survival." Just the way he was, he thought. Animals' tricks worked. Would his?

As she walked out of the swamp, Peanuts stuck a wild daisy through a braid of her hair. It matched the false daisies flopping on her wide-brim hat. A meadowlark flashed yellow as it flew past. Insects murmured complaints about the heat.

"What's a hussy?" Peanuts asked Shortning. He carried the empty basket on the dusty hot lane.

He said, "I saw her in the newspaper at Hopkins's. A hussy is a thin white lady with a long face and a pull-down hat."

"And who's Hitler?" she asked.

"I think he's a baseball player on a white team."

Peanuts pointed to a house in the distance. "Oh, oh, we got

to pass them ladies to reach Sadie in the back of Mrs. Clara Davis's house. Got to pick up Mama's laundry there."

Shortning slowed. Sunshine shimmered like a mirage of gold in the dust before them. "Does Mrs. Davis owe Mama money?"

"Yeah, and there she is."

He smiled. "How much?"

"Oh, five or seven dollars. But don't say nothing, Shortning. Her younger sister's married to the Wilson brothers' nephew, and she could get us shut off the plantation. Get us put out of our sharecropper cabin."

Peanuts glanced at her brother. As he practiced the words he would say, he was thinking that he hadn't felt the struggles of life as a colored child so keenly until after Daddy was sent to the chain gang. So many people were unfair to them. They were at the mercy of the Wilson brothers, at the mercy of Mrs. Clara Davis, at the mercy of the sheriff. . . .

But there was always a way. Not a head-on way like Daddy's, but a tricking way, like the wood duck's. He liked to fool people, but at the same time he hated it. Guilt made him feel dishonest. Was it wrong to trick?

"Shortning," Peanuts warned, "Mama say don't let your mouth get us in trouble!"

E I G H T

🦋

AS HE AND PEANUTS walked near, Shortning acted as if he didn't see the ladies. Five of them, wearing colorful loose housedresses, hats, and summer sandals, straddled the heat, fanning themselves. Perspiration dripped from wisps of hair at foreheads and necks. Their faces were caked with white face powder soaked in sweat. They were sharpening their tongues on gossip.

Holding the laundry basket on a hip, Shortning asked, "Is this where Mrs. Clara Davis live, Sister?" He rubbed his head with his free hand, then placed his tan felt hat respectfully under his arm.

"Yes, Brother," she said. She looked at the dirt lane.

"Wowee! House sure is some pretty!"

Peanuts touched his elbow to remind him that Mrs. Clara Davis was present among the ladies. Peanuts looked down and began to rub her skirt. Her hands shook slightly.

Three feet from the hushed group of ladies, Shortning stopped. Peanuts hastily took the laundry basket from him. He held his hat across his chest in reverence. The audience was better than he could have asked for.

"Toad in the mud," he muttered. "No wonder Mrs. Clara Davis can't pay our mama her ten dollars owed. Our daddy's on the chain gang for something everybody knew he didn't do, and the FBI is coming to ask about him. But, living in a fine white house with a fine white porch and a fine red roof, she can't pay no mind to us poor colored people. Now can she, Sister?"

"Brother, Mrs. Clara Davis is a nice lady. She just forgot is all."

"Yeah, living in a fine white house with a fine white porch and a fine red roof can make a nice lady forget. Ain't that right, Sister?" They walked up to the yard.

The hushed ladies parted like the waters of the Red Sea.

"Excuse me," Peanuts said. She carried the laundry basket past the staring ladies. Her brother followed at a shuffle.

But Shortning Bread wasn't finished. He mumbled, almost under his breath, but loud enough for all to hear, "Mama gonna wash clothes late in the night after chopping cotton beside our brothers all day in the hot sun. And she can't get no pay for it. Mrs. Davis owe her ten whole dollars. But Mrs. Davis is a nice lady living in a fine white house with a . . ."

As he spoke, hairs rose on the back of his neck. It was all true. Comfortable people didn't want to be bothered.

His voice trailed off as Peanuts led him to the backyard. "It was about seven dollars," she whispered.

He whispered, "Ask for ten, get five."

They heard Mrs. Clara Davis hustle to her front door.

At the rear door Peanuts passed the laundry basket to the maid, Sadie, a friend of their family.

Sadie asked, "How you doing, Peanuts?"

"We fine. Shortning Bread was twelve yesterday."

"No kidding," Sadie said. "Happy birthday!"

Her grin showed gaps between pearly white teeth. Her brown skin glistened like satin. Sadie smiled at Shortning.

"I suppose you took the day off? I hear the FBI is coming to ask about your daddy?" She lowered her voice. "Around these parts where white people know colored folks by what we wear, you might need a change of clothes one day." She winked. "Fool folks, you know. Remember our church charity box."

He nodded. He knew Sadie from Sundays at church. She was secretary to the minister.

"That's fine. Be good children now. Your mama's suffering enough with Mr. Rufus gone. And him such a fine Christian man. Didn't even drink no liquor! Don't you children go and break your mama's heart now, you hear?"

Mrs. Clara Davis opened the door into the kitchen just as Sadie said that. She had brought the dirty laundry with money on top. She jerked the bill off the full basket.

"Wait," she said. She huffed herself back into the parlor.

When she returned, she replaced the one bill with a handful, and Sadie passed the laundry basket to Peanuts. There were ten one-dollar bills on top of the dirty clothes. Sadie raised her eyebrows and took off her apron. Her workday was done.

"Thank you, Mrs. Davis," Peanuts called.

Shortning pocketed the money.

As the door shut behind Mrs. Davis, Sadie whispered, "Well, it's about time she paid. Claudia deserve her money. Working days and washing clothes nights." She patted Peanuts's shoulder. "I still remember how tiny you was, child. Born two months too early out in the cotton fields, and gasping for every breath. I was there. Truly you was no bigger than a peanut!" She laughed and hugged Peanuts. They all walked out together, but she went toward the back.

"Good-bye, Miss Sadie," they called.

As they closed the white picket gate, they saw Hawk Baker hiding in a crape myrtle bush across the dusty lane. His knickers kept sliding down over leg socks, and he jerked them up. Shortning thought Hawk's legs must be terribly hot.

All the ladies had disappeared, their tongues sharpened with more to gossip about.

"Are you following us?" Shortning Bread called. His suspender strap flipped against his brown leg. At least he was bare-legged and barefoot in this awful heat.

"I want to know where you live," Hawk said. He stuck hands in his pockets and hunched his shoulders.

"Go home, Mr. Hawk," Shortning called.

As they trotted away, Hawk waved a fist at them. "You'll be sorry, Shortning Bread Jackson!"

Shortning let Peanuts go ahead. Was Hawk threatening him? Did that white boy dare threaten him? He turned and caught up with Hawk and backed him into a swamp. He slipped behind a cypress so no one could see him from the lane. Did this white boy realize what their life in Mississippi was like?

"Do you love your daddy?" he asked Hawk.

"Sure do."

"Do you know where my daddy is?"

"Yeah."

"I love my daddy same as you love yours. And he ain't never done nothing wrong. Do you know that?"

Hawk stepped on one foot, then on the other. He put his hands in his pockets, then took them out. He rubbed his cheek with his knuckles.

He said, "We all know he didn't steal that car. That's what." After he said it, he covered his mouth and glanced over his shoulder.

"Sometimes I think Mississippi is one big trap of meanness," Shortning said, leaning a shoulder against the tree. "My daddy used to call it the 'system.' I call it the 'trap.' And you and me are caught in that trap." He shook his head slowly.

"Seems you'd forget him," Hawk said with a shrug. "Been a couple of years, ain't it?"

Shortning glared at him. "Would you forget your daddy?" He stood straight, turned, and trudged away to catch up with Peanuts.

Hawk's mouth hung open, his eyebrows were raised, and his hands dangled limply, as he stared after Shortning.

NINE

W EDNESDAY MORNING AFTER milk delivery Shortning Bread Jackson was so nervous he could hardly walk home. He didn't go to chop cotton. His brothers did his work without complaint. Even Elias seemed to sense he was about something big and needed time off. When he passed the sheriff's house, he saw that the trellis was finished. Someone was painting it with thin white primer. Would the trellis be white or blue? he wondered.

As he walked, his legs felt like pig jelly, and his lungs fairly burst. Jude was all set to change the sign. Shortning, himself, had piled boxes beside Hopkins's general store, a hiding place for him and Peanuts. Now all he needed to do was pray. When he reached home, he stretched out on his bed. The musty wood floor smelled like home.

How would this work out? He put hands behind his head and crossed his feet. Jude knew the whole plan now, but he hadn't told Elias. Instead, Jude had promised to deliver a white man to the general store on River Road by noon. Noon today.

Shortning hoped Jude found a tall white man to send. Sheriff Titus Clark towered over most folks in town. He had long lanky legs and an impressive chest and shoulders. That was probably why they hired him as sheriff. His looks made a thief think twice.

The sheriff's eyes could be pale blue and angry like painful-cold ice, yet warm and merry when he played Santa Claus. He was balding, and seemed embarrassed about it. Folks said he hadn't always worn his sheriff hat in the heat. Only since he was bald did he sport the full uniform, hat and all. Sweat ran down his neck and forehead, but he kept his bald spot covered. He didn't even cut holes in his hat!

When Peanuts came home for Shortning, they walked into town together. She kept folding and unfolding her arms, and sometimes she skipped ahead of him.

By 11:30, using a shortcut to town, they trotted to the side of Hopkins's store to watch from their nest. The sky was overcast; the air was hot and humid like a duck-down pillow over the face.

Sheriff Titus Clark drove up in his car. He parked under a tree and opened the doors. So he had really fallen for it! Shortning shook his head. How dumb could some grown-ups be? Guilty consciences must blind and deafen people. The sheriff sat with one long, lanky leg out in the dust.

Mr. Tom Turner drove by on the tomato truck. He looked at Sheriff Clark sitting there. Another truck with colored workers slowed by the store and parked. When the sheriff stood to stare at them, the white drivers grinned and both trucks rolled away.

A neighbor pulled up with mule and wagon. He let his mule drink at the horse trough. A horse-drawn cart pulled up beside him, and the two colored drivers began whispering.

Sheriff Clark opened the neck of his shirt a button, then rebuttoned it. His leg outside the car began to twitch, and he drew it in.

At that moment Shortning Bread Jackson realized the explosive possibility of what was taking place. Anything could happen. An innocent stranger might even be murdered at a meeting with this nervous sheriff. And Shortning would feel responsible. He didn't want any more tragedy. What had he done? All he wanted was to free his daddy. Shortning looked at Peanuts. Her eyes were as big as pancakes. She pointed.

Along with other ladies, Mrs. Abigail Middleton sat fanning herself in the shade of a neighbor's porch. She called to a friend returning with green beans from the store.

"Come set a spell with me."

Her friend acted surprised, but scrambled eagerly onto the porch. "What you doing here, Abigail? Let me tell you about this book I'm reading, *Gone with the Wind*. Just came out. Tells all about the South when we were all rich, and the Negroes worked as proper slaves. Those were the days."

Her voice was loud. Shortning's heart sank. It was clear where her sympathy lay. He swallowed and his throat felt closed. Everywhere people of Sleepy Corners gathered in groups, whispering and staring. Waiting for the FBI agent.

No, the stranger wouldn't be in danger with all those witnesses around. But you never could tell about white folks in Sleepy Corners. They covered for one another. They let his daddy go to the chain gang when they knew better. Why, he had been delivering milk for many of them at the exact time the car was smashed! But then again, his daddy was colored. Colored people didn't matter very much in Mississippi.

The church clock began striking twelve. In the distance Shortning heard a car motor humming. A new car motor, not a local junker, or a truck motor. His heart began to pound. Toad in the mud, Jude had delivered on the hour!

The car was a new, black, two-door Ford. The man inside drove slowly, staring from one side of the road to the other.

Sheriff Titus Clark stood and swayed slightly, or was it the heat that made it seem that way? He hitched his long-legged pants, and stuck his thumbs in his belt. The shirt of his uniform was wet and dark. He strode over to the car, and the driver stopped.

"Yes, sir," said Titus Clark. "I been waiting for you."

The man looked the sheriff up and down. He seemed at ease; he even smiled.

"Afternoon, Sheriff." He pointed. "Do people congregate here on a daily basis? Or is there an occasion I should know about?"

Toad in the mud, thought Shortning. This man used big words. The car had different auto tags, not Mississippi-color tags. Even when they were covered with dust, he knew Mississippi tags. Were the tags from a northern state? He held his breath.

The sheriff turned toward the lanes and porches, and people suddenly looked away and moved their mouths in talk. Five or six ladies sat by Mrs. Middleton. Groups of white men stood under trees, leaned against the store, sat on porches.

Arms folded, red-haired Mrs. Priscilla Hopkins stood outside her store. She wore a smug smile, and her jaw was jutted out. Mr. Horse Face Hopkins peered from inside.

"Sir," the sheriff answered, "these here people are law-abiding citizens minding their own business!" His voice was louder than at first. He seemed to be feeling more confident, maybe even growing angry.

The stranger opened the door to his car. Sheriff Titus Clark quickly moved aside, almost with a bow. The stranger stepped out and seemed shorter than when he was sitting.

Oh, no! Shortning covered his face. The man was so short, he looked like a midget. He must have been sitting on a cushion.

"I suppose," the driver said, stretching arms and rubbing his neck, "I suppose this is Sleepy Corners and not Lewis Lands?"

"Yes, sir!" said the sheriff, staring down at the man. He seemed embarrassed, almost bewildered, about the man's size.

Peanuts shook Shortning's arm. He heard footsteps in the dramatic summer silence and looked around. Mr. Bill Brown swayed his stocky body around the corner of the lane and aimed straight for the store. He weaved a drunken path, stopped, caught a tree to keep from falling.

"Is that the man, Titus?" he called in a loud, slurred voice.

Peanuts and Shortning giggled silently. Toad in the mud!

The mail truck drove up behind the stranger as Mr. Bill Brown plowed toward them. Mr. Charlie Baker didn't have Hawk inside this time. He got out and put a hand on the sheriff's shoulder. They both stared at the strange driver.

The driver ran a finger around his collar. He pointed. "I'm going for a cool limeade over at the store, if you gentlemen will pardon me."

"I'll be waiting right here," said the sheriff.

After the man toddled to the store on tiny feet, Postmaster Baker began talking earnestly in a low voice to the sheriff. Titus Clark struck his fist in his hand.

"No!" he shouted. "I did my duty!"

People stopped murmuring and stared. With a frown the sheriff looked around at everyone and hitched his pants. He seemed to be daring someone for a fight.

Shortning heard a scuffle inside the general store. Mr. Bill called, "Where the money hid, mister? Where's the bottle? Stand still, mister. Hey, don't push me."

Peanuts covered her face and shook in silent laughter.

Mrs. Priscilla Hopkins screeched, "Sheriff, come keep the peace. Mr. Bill Brown's bothering this gentleman."

The sheriff strode over. Charlie Baker jumped in his mail truck and drove off.

More scuffling and drunken words from the general store: "But I know he hid money. I heard about it. There's bottles too." Sheriff Clark walked out holding Mr. Bill Brown by the collar and the seat of his pants.

The driver toddled out carrying a paper cup. "Thank you for handling that, Sheriff," he said. "I'm sure you'll take care of everything wisely."

Shortning raised eyebrows at Peanuts.

Sheriff Clark's face was red. He said nothing.

Hopping in his car, the stranger turned and backed, turned and backed again, took his hand off the wheel and waved to the people. Everyone waved back at him. Then grinning, he drove off slowly, swirling the ice, sipping his cold limeade.

Shortning's heart sank. He felt as if nothing had happened. He was right back where he started. But what did he expect?

Sheriff Titus Clark slid into his car, gunned the motor, and roared away. Mrs. Abigail Middleton carried her rocker off the neighbor's porch, followed by her friends carrying their chairs. They formed a parade of middle-aged ladies in loose housedresses carrying wicker rocking chairs. Men in front of the general store slapped hats on heads and faded away.

Peanuts was smiling. She pointed to the dust from the sheriff's car. "I don't know how you did it, but you did it, Shortning Bread Jackson!"

Really? She still thought it was an FBI agent? Now what? Shortning wondered.

T E N

O N THURSDAY, AFTER A morning rain, Shortning
helped Peanuts get another late payment and bring
clothes from town. When they reached their cabin, surround-
ed by fields of young green cotton, Shortning filled the galvanized washtub with clear cold water from the pump. The
one field pump provided water for two dozen sharecropper
cabins. The Jacksons washed clothes outside in the shade of
the house.

Peanuts held out her hand. "I'll put the money in the
lard can."

Shortning unfolded some money. "Five dollars today, thir-
teen dollars Tuesday," he said. "I made up for not chopping
cotton."

After she heard about what Shortning did, his proud
mama gave him more time off from chopping cotton. He
didn't just have a day off, he had a week! Mama was
impressed that Shortning had made the FBI in Washington
send an agent all the way to Sleepy Corners in Mississippi.
Elias had been a bit doubtful about it all, but Jude had
grinned and said, "Sure, let him have a few days off. Not too
much to be done right now."

"Mama be happy," Peanuts said. She stared at the money,
sighed, and said: "Mama ain't got hopes up for Daddy, but

she want to get ahead some. In Chicago they paying seventy-five cents an hour for laundry work, hotel work, mail order work. Plenty of work there for coloreds. Before Daddy left, I heard him saying there's a train from Clarksdale to Memphis, and another from Memphis to Chicago called the Illinois Central. And train fare is ten dollars for a one-way ticket."

"Ten dollars?" Shortning said. "And there's seven of us?"

"I know. But the slaves used to walk. We can walk too."

She climbed the ladder and stepped over the doorsill. After she hid the money, she returned, unwrapping a bar of soap.

"How much else in there?" he asked.

"Just fifteen dollars."

"We have to eat," Shortning said abruptly. He had felt proud of all the money he had collected, but now it seemed like nothing. His shoulders drooped and he closed his eyes.

Life seemed like a trap for poor colored people. Here the sheriff spent money to paint his house, when it didn't need painting. He spent money buying fancy dresses for his daughter's wedding. But the Jacksons had to beg for their proper pay to buy food, and their daddy was sent to the chain gang unfairly.

Peanuts said, "I'll spot and scrub the clothes."

Shortning climbed into the house, ready to play some music and rest. Inside the door he turned and looked at his sister, who worked so hard. Down on the ground she was sorting colors of clothes. Black and brown went in two buckets of water, light colors and white she dunked in the big washtub.

Women's work is hard, he thought, but men's path is even rougher. Look at my daddy. I'm a boy now, but when I'm a man, I'll be poor with a poor wife and hungry children; I might be jailed for something I never did; I might be beaten, or shot, or lynched to keep "coloreds in their place." How can I escape? I'm trapped!

Climbing down, he went over to Peanuts. "Let me help."

She pointed. "There's a piece of soap there. Look for dirt spots. Wet them, rub soap, and scrub them. Get all the collars and cuffs and under arms."

He began to imitate her. This was wet, messy work. Squatting hurt his back, and he was sweating. Dirty clothes smelled under arms and in crotches. This was handling some white people's smelly dirt, and his mother and sister did it almost every evening. Something stuck in his throat and his eyes burned, then grew watery. He stared into the tub of gray scum.

Calling, "Hi y'all doing?" noisy children ran past, carrying tin lunch pails to their fathers and mothers in the cotton fields. Shortning sniffed corn bread, red beans and rice, and baked sweet potatoes in the pails. He watched the little children running. Peanuts pointed toward the lane.

"Oh, no," she said, "look who found us."

Hands in pockets, Hawk Baker picked his path toward them through clots of runny mud. Shortning felt a flush of shame at being found doing women's work, but he gritted his teeth. His mama and sister earned money for his food and his schoolbooks and his winter shoes this way. Why shouldn't he wash clothes for once too?

It was lunchtime and his stomach ached from hunger. Toad in the mud!

Hawk called, "I found you. Now I know which cabin you Jacksons live in."

Shortning spotted and scrubbed under arms on Mrs. Clara Davis's dress, and the hurt was unbearable. The pain in his throat ached in his heart too. Would they have to live like this forever?

Hawk squatted near Shortning, but his thighs were too thick, so he plopped flat on the ground. His gray eyes were sparkling.

Shortning sighed and looked up. "Mr. Hawk, you should-n't be here. Folks down by the river don't like white boys coming by. Now that you know where we live, please go home!"

"I see Sheriff Clark's staying in his house today. That FBI man must have worried him."

Peanuts slowed her spotting. Shortning raised his eye-brows.

Hawk said, "I was figuring that maybe my daddy and me could go see about your daddy. I wouldn't let the sheriff stop me."

Peanuts and Shortning stopped working and stared at him.

Hawk laughed. "We're white and my daddy's the postmas-ter. Maybe we could do something."

Shortning thought: Were Hawk and his daddy the people with influence who could get his daddy freed? In a snap? Here it was Thursday, one day after his "FBI man" arrived—thanks to Jude—and already something was happening.

Peanuts sped up. Shortning did too. "All right, Mr. Hawk," he said. "Go do something. And I'll say thank you!"

"Can I see in your house first?"

Shortning glared at Hawk. "What you think you'll find?"

Hawk flushed pink. "Well, I don't know. I don't live in a sharecropper cabin. And I have a piano."

They had finished spotting dirt. Peanuts pushed all the clothes to soak under water, squeezing air pockets.

"Well, I don't have a piano." Shortning jumped up. He did have something to show Hawk after all; he wanted to show Hawk his music. "But come on," he said, waving Hawk up the rickety wooden ladder to the cabin.

"Why?" Hawk asked, pointing to logs raising the house.

"Low land. Mighty Miss flood here 'most every spring." Where Hawk lived was high land in town. Hawk didn't have to worry about floods.

"Oh." Shortning watched Hawk stare at the handful of Rhode Island Red chickens picking insects out of dirt.

When Hawk climbed over the doorsill, Shortning waved to the one room. A sheet hung over a clothes line that divided the room into a sleeping area and an eating area. A half dozen crates were used as chairs around a sturdy wooden table near the wood-burning stove.

Church clothes were hung neatly on nails in the wooden walls. Mattresses sewn from flour sacks and stuffed with Spanish moss were arranged on the floor. The family picked the moss off live oak and cypress trees, dried it in the sun, and stuffed their mattresses. Peanuts slept with Mama now, but Shortning never looked at that mattress without remembering helping Mama wake Daddy up in the mornings.

His mama always said Rufus Jackson was a dead serious sleeper! And that sleeping so much might be why he was such a dreamer! A dreamer with plans he couldn't carry out.

But Shortning wanted to show Hawk something else. He pulled spoons out of a drawer in the table. Fitting spoon handles between fingers, he began to play ragtime music on the spoons, flicking them together, his hand resting on a knee. He hummed to harmonize with the clicking sounds.

Hawk stared and listened. "Hey, I know that song. What's the name of it?"

Shortning straightened up. He looked at his spoons and shrugged. "You should know. I learned it from you."

"You listen to me play?" Hawk laughed. He sat gingerly on a crate. "Sure, then that's Scott Joplin's 'Maple Leaf Rag.'"

Shortning stared at his spoons. "You make music on piano, and I make music on spoons. See, we're alike." He was joking. Staring at the battered spoons, he felt his spoon music was silly, but Hawk Baker had a real piano.

Peanuts heard as she topped the ladder. Proudly she said, "He used to have bones. They sounded some fine!"

Shortning's face brightened. "Greatest set of matched rib bones, all dry, and they made a great sound." He grinned at his wiggling toes. "Until a friend's dog chewed my bones." They all laughed.

Peanuts cleared her throat. She rested a hand on Mama's bean pot and looked at her brother. With Hawk there, what would they do about eating lunch?

E L E V E N

❧

*I*T WAS ABOUT LUNCHTIME on Thursday. Shortning
talked to Hawk about piano music, while his thoughts
were on that pot of red beans set back on the stove for him
and Peanuts.

"I listen outside your house," he said. "I like your music
playing."

Staring at Peanuts, he thought of all the times white people
ate in front of him, and never offered him any food. Times
while he and his brothers cut grass, or while he and his
brothers painted walls, or while he and his brothers washed
windows. Now here was Hawk Baker. How would they
treat him?

He remembered his daddy saying white folks just didn't
think colored folks got hungry. "They don't even notice us,"
he said once. "I worked all day for that man with him drinking water and eating cheese and bread, and he never offered
me nothing. I almost fainted walking home."

"Toad in the mud," Shortning said with a sigh. His mama
would say, "Two wrongs don't make a right." He reached for
three speckled-blue tin plates.

"Mr. Hawk, have you eaten anything?"

"No." Hawk sat up straighter. "My mama's gone with my
daddy."

Shortning held out his hand; Peanuts gave him a spoon. She pointed to the red beans; the pot was almost empty. He spooned up some, added a plop of cold rice, and handed it to Hawk. Peanuts took a baked sweet potato left for them on the back of the stove. She cut it into three pieces and gave the thickest center piece to Hawk.

Hawk ate the red beans, then nibbled at the sweet potato, turning his head from side to side, watching how they ate.

Shortning couldn't control himself. He wolfed down the red beans. Inwardly he moaned because in sharing, they each had less food. Shortning gobbled the mealy rich sweet potato, skin, stem, and all. He had hoped to eat slowly to make the food last until his stomach reported to his head that he had eaten, and the rat-chewing, aching hunger eased away, but he couldn't. He just couldn't.

Reaching for the dented aluminum pitcher, he visited the pump. They washed lunch down with tin cups of cold refreshing well water. He suspected the others were still hungry too.

"Now," he said, "we gotta leave, Mr. Hawk."

As one after another the three of them climbed down the ladder and trotted across the uneven field, Negro neighbors looked out doorways with frightened expressions. Whispering children gathered in worried groups like hens when the fox is at the henhouse door. Shortning decided to try to explain later about Hawk Baker's visit. He sure hoped he wasn't getting his family into trouble.

At the lane Shortning pointed. "Mr. Hawk, you go that way. We'll take the lane over yonder. Ain't no need to be seen together. It would just worry folks and cause us trouble."

"But I'm alone," Hawk said, and held his breath.

"I know."

Hawk put hands in pockets. "That was nice." He looked at Shortning Bread. "I like your music too."

As a car drove closer, Shortning slipped into the field bordering the lane and bent over to hide. "You still can't shake my hand," he told Hawk, although he knew he shouldn't be mocking him. That wouldn't be kind. He hoped he was just talking about it, just saying what was true. He didn't want to be caught in that trap of Mississippi meanness.

"We're not equal," Hawk said. "I live"—he waved toward Sleepy Corners—"there, and . . ."

"I live there," said Shortning. He gestured toward his cabin. He crouched with Peanuts behind tall staked tomato plants in the wet field near the lane where Hawk stood.

"I play piano."

"I play spoons, and sometimes bones."

"I eat different food for lunch."

Quickly Shortning answered, "I eat lunch too."

"I sleep in a bed."

"So do I," said Shortning with a scowl.

"You call that pad on the floor a bed?"

Peanuts squeezed Shortning Bread's hand as a warning.

"So we're not equal," Hawk said, walking along the lane parallel to the path where Shortning and Peanuts crept in the field. Hawk took his hands from his pockets and looked at them. "Besides, I'm white."

Shortning raised his hands. "And I'm brown. Tell me, what color do you bleed?"

Hawk stared at his hands and put them back in his pockets. Without another word Shortning Bread and Peanuts cut across the muddy tomato field to a back lane.

They arrived in town first, and in front of the general store a half dozen white men talked with Horace Hopkins.

"You think FDR be reelected in the fall?" one asked.

"Not the way he running this country," said another.

"Got a lot of enemies." The speaker scratched his head.

"On the other hand," a frecklefaced man said, "Roosevelt's trying to put people back to work. Now take Mississippi, they saying we need more industry."

Peanuts strolled past them, followed by Shortning.

"Industry?" called a man spitting in the dust. "If we take them industries, we take them northerners telling us how to live. Telling us how to treat our niggers—like that FBI man. I say cotton's all the industry we need."

The frecklefaced man said, "A one-crop state lives by one crop, and when that crop fail . . ."

"We always got tomatoes."

"And they ain't buying them," a man said. "We in some hard times, a bad depression they saying."

"Mississippi always . . . always . . . have hard times," Horace Hopkins said, staring across River Road.

Peanuts and Shortning stood under a dripping tree. "Hawk better go straight home with my red beans and sweet potato in his white-boy stomach," Peanuts said. "He better get his daddy to help our daddy."

"I think he'll do it," Shortning said. "You know what? I think he's . . . nice. You know what I mean? For a white boy, that is."

"It's just Thursday. This week ain't over, Abraham Lincoln Jackson," she warned. "We ain't heard the last of Mr. Hawk Baker's sweet-talking ways."

"I wonder," he said. A tan butterfly rested on a wildflower

cluster. He noticed the butterfly had pale spots on tan and blended in color with the flower.

"What?"

"I wonder how'd he get the name of Hawk?"

"See there!" she said. "You know Daddy says hawks kill pigeons and brown sparrows." She sighed. "I hope he don't get our family into more trouble. Look!"

Walking down River Road, Hawk Baker strolled toward the general store. One of the men out front pointed. He called:

"Ain't that Charlie Baker's boy what drowned this past Monday morning? I was wondering if they found the body for a funeral?"

No one answered. The men all stared and rubbed their stubby beards, or lifted hats and scratched their heads.

Hawk bought a pink lemonade and strolled toward his house while Shortning and Peanuts watched.

ᴵ T WAS ABOUT 1:30 THURSDAY afternoon. Peanuts and Shortning left the tree and walked past Hawk Baker with his pink lemonade showing through the paper cup.

Stores in Mississippi were not allowed to sell colored people food or drink. Peanuts wiped her dry lips, and Shortning swallowed.

Hawk looked over at them and smiled. "I'll be seeing you," he called. Grinning, he stooped and picked up a stone to toss.

A lady carrying a paper bag turned to glare her disapproval at Shortning Bread and Peanuts. Respectfully, they looked down at the muddy lane. The morning rain hadn't dried.

"Why'd she have to look at us?" he muttered to Peanuts. "I didn't say it. Just so he free Daddy, I don't care if I never see Mr. Hawk again in all my born days!"

As soon as he said it, he realized it wasn't true. He would like Hawk as a friend. Hawk was different. Maybe Hawk could help them? Shortning dragged his toes through the mud; it felt squishy, soft, cooling.

But Hawk couldn't be a friend; Shortning knew that too. Hawk was white and Shortning was black. That lady who frowned at him and Peanuts just now, she knew. If Hawk Baker tried to visit Shortning Bread Jackson too often, the

Jacksons would be shot or burned to teach them a lesson. Hawk's parents would be warned, scolded, called nigger lovers.

As if she knew what he was thinking, Peanuts took his hand. They trudged home slowly.

Passing the sheriff's house, Shortning saw that the trellis was painted blue and white crisscrossing. A long, narrow table was set up, and there were wooden lawn chairs on the grass. They seemed to have been borrowed from different neighbors.

Shortning wondered what Hawk and his daddy could do to free Rufus. Maybelle Clark was marrying at the end of next week. That meant the sheriff would be laying low for just one more week.

All day Friday Shortning Bread Jackson worked like a beaver with a dam to build. He sawed and split logs for the wood-burning stove. He aired all the mattresses in hot sanitizing sunshine. He helped Peanuts deliver and return with laundry.

On hands and knees he scrubbed the cabin floor with soap and a red clay brick. Grease droppings from cooking and mattress markings disappeared; and when the floor dried, it had a spotless rosy glow. With a broom he swept spiderwebs and wasp nests from the cabin walls and rafters.

Butterflies fluttered past and katydids and walkingsticks moved nearby, and Shortning never noticed them.

Seemingly inspired by her brother, Peanuts washed, rinsed, and hung Mrs. Ogles's clothes instead of leaving them for her mother to do. Colorful clothes waved gently on lines in sunlight like a row of snapdragons gently swaying in a garden.

* * *

It was dusk Friday and Peanuts was boiling starch for dress collars and men's shirts when she spied the family arriving from the cotton fields. She called Shortning. Elias walked beside his mama. They stepped in as the thin wisp of a new moon rose high. Elias and James hung their hats. Jude came from washing up at the pump and winked at Shortning.

There was a Friday night dance at Mt. Olivet AME Church, but Shortning's brothers never attended dances anymore. Not since their daddy was sent to the chain gang. Elias and James patted Shortning on the shoulder.

The family was still in hushed awe at Shortning, calling and delivering the FBI to Sleepy Corners!

Peanuts held out the lard can, and Claudia saw the money collected. She saw the drying clothes, the clean cabin, the bubbling starch. She could only say, "My, my, my!"

She barely had time to say it when Elias raised his head. James put a finger behind his ear. Jude, who was brushing his hair, stopped. Shortning Bread and Peanuts stared at each other. They had heard somebody whistle.

Claudia Jackson clutched her heart with both hands. She shuddered and swayed in the hot air as if she might faint, but in moments she planted her bare feet surely. She squared her shoulders and sighed.

"That ain't what it sounds like," Peanuts said in a squeaky voice. "But it sure did sound like Daddy."

The whistle repeated. It was louder this time, and a truck motor droned closer as well. Claudia held on to the table.

"It is Daddy!" shouted Shortning. He leaped out the door, fell to the ground, rolled, and stood up to run, then raced into darkness.

Peanuts winced and covered her face with both hands. The family could hear Shortning's footsteps drumming across the field. Peanuts shook her head and sighed.

Claudia Jackson turned to the stove, picked up the matchbox, and put it down again. She pulled a cooking pot from the corner and climbed down the ladder. Head down, she trudged wearily toward the field pump, where several women already stood in line.

The truck's two headlights were blinding as it churned through soft ground. Shortning Bread was shouting now. Elias climbed down and ran to catch his mother and bring her back. Jude and James guarded the bottom of the ladder. Families all around them ran back to their cabins and stood in uneasy groups.

Elias, Jude, and James stood around their mother like pioneers circling the wagons for safety. No colored man—except maybe the funeral director with his hearse and a preacher from Natchez—owned a truck. This could be Mississippi chariot coming.

In the distance Shortning Bread chanted, "Daddy, Daddy, Daddy!" Peanuts saw that he was standing on the running board and clinging to the side of the truck. She sat in the raised doorsill above her mother's head. Her hands clutched the wood until her knuckles were sharp bumps.

When the truck pulled to a stop, a door swung open. Shortning Bread jumped off and dragged a thin, ragged man out of the back. Postmaster Charlie Baker sat in the driver's seat, with Hawk squeezed between him and his smiling wife.

Rufus Jackson stumbled over to his wife and held her in a hungry hug. The older sons and Peanuts were frozen in space, but Shortning danced up and down.

He called, "Daddy's free!"

Families around them began to move again, shifting back into evening chores: lighting wood with kindling, waiting for water at the pump, peeling onions. Girls and children smiled and nodded for the Jacksons. However, some men frowned and hitched their pants nervously. Some women clutched their babies and called young children inside like mother hens hiding chicks under their wings.

Peanuts climbed down the ladder and dragged her frozen brothers forward to greet their daddy. In the headlights they saw what two years on the Mississippi chain gang had done to him. Painfully thin, he looked twenty years older than when he had left. Sunken eyes seemed to be wells in his wrinkled, smiling face. And welts and running sores covered his arms.

Claudia Jackson and her children laughed and cried and laughed again as they hugged Rufus Jackson. They all called thanks to the Bakers over and over. Without saying a word or getting out, Mr. Charlie Baker made a slow circle with his truck, then began to drive back toward the road, the truck wobbling in loose dirt. But before he got too far away, he stopped. Hawk jumped out and ran toward Shortning Bread.

With his back to the truck, Hawk was lit only by the new moon. He held out his hand. Shortning Bread stared at Hawk's hand for several seconds, then stared at Hawk.

He felt resentful toward this white boy, resentful toward all the white people who thought he wasn't as good as they were. Should he accept Hawk's hand? Did this mean that Hawk thought they were equals?

Their fathers could not see them; their mothers could not

see them; their friends could not see them. No old ladies could frown. No sheriff was around.

There in the dark of a wishful new Mississippi moon, Shortning Bread Jackson and Hawk Baker shook hands.

THIRTEEN

❦

HAT FRIDAY NIGHT, WITH soulful eyes and soft voices, neighbors hugged his daddy. One of Shortning's friends said, "We glad you got your daddy back. For the time being."

Women silently hugged Claudia, then patted her shoulder and walked away. Even dogs tucked their tails and crept away from the Jackson cabin.

When everyone had walked away, Rufus Jackson said, "Peanuts and Shortning Bread, you two children go on to the Brewsters' cabin now. We got to have a talk."

"Daddy," Shortning said, "I'm twelve years old now." Peanuts slid her foot beside his. "And Peanuts is grown too," he added. "We want to stay."

"Let them be," Claudia said.

Rufus touched them, each bony-fingered hand resting on a head in fatherly blessing. "You some fine-looking children," he said. He looked at his three older sons. "All of you. I'm so proud of you!"

Firelight flickered from the open door of the stove and lit the room. The cheerful light chased shadows around the walls. Shortning looked at his brothers.

James, short and thin, stood looking out the window from time to time. His hair was dusty from the cotton field. He

77

was bare chested and dressed in blue denim overalls. One trembling hand clutched the sill of the window.

Next to him Jude stood with arms folded tightly. He faced the open door and kept glancing into the distance. Shortning wondered if Annie Lou was waiting for him. Jude had washed up and changed into gray pants and a light green short-sleeved shirt. One bare foot kept scratching the other.

Did Jude wish he was at the Friday night dance with Annie Louise? Now Shortning's brothers could go again. Daddy was home. But how long would they be in Mississippi?

Elias was the oldest. Broad shouldered, he sat on a crate nearest his daddy, the place of honor among the children. His elbows pressed tensely on his knees.

Shortning drew a sharp breath. This was the whole family together again. He grinned, and Peanuts squeezed his hand.

Rufus began: "I learned a lot on that chain gang. Most of which I hope you'll never have to know." He sat on a crate.

Shortning's grin faded.

"But one thing you all got to learn is why they treat us colored folks the way they do. Listen to me now. Out of every ten people in Mississippi, seven are us. Negro. Seven coloreds to every three whites. That's what throws fear into the whites. That's why they have to keep us down."

Claudia nodded. She pushed the bubbling starch off the burner and sat on a crate on the other side of Rufus. Peanuts handed her two flatirons to heat on the stove. They had ironing to do that night.

Rufus stared at the irons and said, "For over two hundred years of slavery, they disgraced our women, worked us men to death, and starved our children. Now they scared. They need our labor, and they fear our freedom."

Elias said, "Amen, Daddy." James and Jude nodded. Shortning sat beside Peanuts on his mattress.

A thump shook the cabin, and a shrill squeal startled them. The family dived for the floor. Only their daddy, face in hands, sat still on his crate.

After a moment of quiet, Elias leaped up and jumped out the door. Shortning closed his eyes and felt perspiration drip off his face. He smelled sweat from James's body next to his. Soon Elias's footsteps creaked on the ladder.

Shortning opened his eyes and saw Elias with a pink-and-black piglet under his arm. Shortning covered his face in shame. He felt he had been a coward. Elias grinned broadly. The family crawled off the floor.

Elias said, "Little piggy here tried to scratch her back on the post and got a nasty splinter."

Rufus took the squealing pig on his lap and scratched its neck tenderly. Peanuts knelt by her daddy, and Shortning stood looking over his shoulder. Their daddy was back and helping animals again. He used to tie broken wings to heal and feed baby birds fallen from nests. He used to wrap dogs' broken legs, using sticks as splints until they knit.

With a penknife Rufus gently removed a long, sharp splinter. Claudia dipped a rag in water and cleaned the cut. She pressed to stop the bleeding. By the time they gave the piglet to its owner, who came to the door, the bleeding had stopped.

When they were alone again, Rufus went on talking: "I'm free now, but you can't make Titus Clark look like a fool and get away with it."

Shortning knew that. Maybelle Clark's wedding was in just one week. They had one week of security from lynchings, beatings, Klan activity—"stirring up" the colored community.

"But I was delivered by the Lord. Tomorrow I would have been dead," Rufus said. "They warned me to say my prayers. Prepare to meet my Maker." He covered his face with his hands.

Claudia reached to squeeze his arm. "Why, Rufus? Why?"

"For telling the truth," he said. "Man from the railroad was out asking about work conditions. Guard told him they fed us three times a day and gave us water twice extra besides. Man asked me if that was true. I stared at his boots until he asked again. I shook my head no."

Claudia stretched both arms around his shoulders.

"I told the truth," he said. "Maybe it was a dumb thing to do, but all I had to cling to was the goodness of the Lord. I try to live by truth. They fed us once in the morning and gave us water once at night."

"That's all?" Claudia asked, her voice shrill.

"Men dropped dead like flies caught in molasses, men clearing land and laying railroad tracks," he said. "Fifty started with me two years ago, and seventeen of us still living. Sickness and weakness killed most of them. Others lost their minds. Went to shouting and struggling. Guards shot them and cut them out of the chains."

Elias stood up, put his hands in his pockets, and paced the floor. James stared out the window. His jaw was twitching. Hands fisted, Jude tightened his folded arms and closed his eyes.

Rufus said, "We got to go north. To Chicago!"

Elias walked over to pull a sheet of paper from his Sunday pants hanging on a nail in the wall. He gave it to his daddy. "They been passing these out in town," he said.

Rufus unfolded the paper and flattened it on the table. He

stared at the words. "Shortning," he said, "read this to your mama."

Shortning stood up slowly. He knew why his daddy called him. His daddy couldn't read, and his mama couldn't read either.

As he read, he touched the words. His mama and daddy followed his finger on the paper.

JOBS IN CHICAGO—MEN AND WOMEN WANTED
HIRING FROM 12TH AND MICHIGAN—ILLINOIS CENTRAL
TRAIN STATION
GOOD PAY
KITCHENETTE APARTMENTS AVAILABLE

Shortning sucked in his breath and squeezed Peanuts's hand until she jerked it away. Chicago! Would they really leave?

F O U R T E E N

THE NEXT MORNING WAS SATURDAY. When his mama woke him, the night before seemed like a dream to Shortning. But Rufus lay sleeping on the mattress. Daddy was really, truly home. Shortning had fallen asleep while the family talked. Already dressed, he leaped off his bed to help Mr. O'Malley.

"Sorry, Mama," he said. He almost never overslept.

She put a finger in his face. "Now you don't tell nobody what we talked about last night," she whispered. "You hear?"

"Yes, ma'am," he said.

On Sunday, for the first time in two years they attended Mt. Olivet AME Church as a whole family. Most people hugged and congratulated them because their daddy was home. A few people seemed nervous around the Jacksons, Shortning thought. Nervous as if they might bring people bad luck.

Monday, Shortning was in a daze. All the excitement had left him exhausted. In the morning he was slow and confused about Mr. O'Malley's milk delivery. Later he dragged his hoe chopping cotton. Cotton field workers' voices rose and fell in songs sung low, but he couldn't sing with them.

Tuesday, when they were in rows side by side, Jude began to talk: "Daddy think we all want to go north. What about my Annie Lou? I can't leave her."

Shortning stopped and stared at Jude. Annie Louise was pretty. Dark brown and plump, she sometimes worked cotton in rows near them. She was a sharecropper neighbor's daughter and loved singing at Mt. Olivet AME. Her voice was sweet and high.

"You ain't going with us? Jude, you can't do that! Daddy won't go without you." He leaned on his hoe.

"Then don't tell him. I just won't go. She my girl. We been saving to get married next year."

"You only seventeen," Shortning said. He took off his hat and fanned his face with it. "You can't marry now."

"We'll both be eighteen then. Mama was fifteen and Daddy seventeen when they married."

Jude was interrupted by a car horn. At the end of the row some white men sat in a Ford car. Among the workers, singing died out until only mosquitoes and cicadas made midday music. Jude and Shortning followed people walking to the Ford.

Both Wilson brothers, faces sweaty and frowning, sprawled in the back of the car. White shirts were open at the necks and they wore yellow straw hats. A tall white man stepped out of the car and read an announcement:

"It has come to our attention that certain illegal persons have been handing out sheets advertising jobs in Chicago.

"There are no jobs for Negroes in Chicago. Furthermore, anyone leaving before the settle in November will be hunted down and put in jail. And in November, only those workers not owing the company money can leave."

The man cleared his throat. "The Wilson brothers have checked their books, and everyone will owe the company this November."

Not one of the two dozen cotton workers made a sound. A breeze rustled leaves to break the sorrowful silence. The white man climbed back into the Ford and drove the Wilson brothers to another area of their plantation. As the car drove out of hearing, people murmured:

"No jobs for Negroes? How do he know?"

"Bad as slavery days. Sharecropping is new slavery."

"Everybody owes, sure! He keep the books. No wonder everybody owes the company."

"Liars!"

Jude and Shortning Bread were silent. Some women groaned. Nearby someone broke down sobbing. Shortning felt his heart pounding.

When they were alone again in their rows, he said: "Daddy won't leave now, and the sheriff will kill him! Maybelle Clark's wedding is in just three days. We have three days to leave safely."

"We don't owe them nothing!" Jude yelled. "Mama and Peanuts wash laundry at night for money."

Shortning caught his brother's arm. "Hush," he said, looking around. "Somebody might tell on us." They returned to silent chopping.

Shortning saw a truck pass. Several times that week Shortning had seen the mail truck pass and Hawk Baker leaning out the window. He had talked to Hawk Baker twice, learning things he needed to know. Now he kept his head down. He'd heard from Peanuts that Hawk wasn't playing with the boys who'd left him to drown.

All week Daddy had slept late mornings. When he awoke, he joined Mama chopping cotton. She cooked extra food to "fill in under his ribs," as she said, but Daddy could hardly eat. His sores stopped running, though, and began to scab over.

Whenever Shortning looked at his daddy, he felt sorrowful sad and crazy angry at the people who had treated him that way. He remembered his strong brown muscular daddy. This dark stranger was a skeleton. But it was Daddy's same spirit that shone through, steady and bright as a candle in a lantern.

And the awful thing was, as Shortning knew, some of those whites who abused colored people were churchgoing, children-loving, sincere people. They just hated colored people.

Wednesday and Thursday evenings the family argued in circles because of the Wilson brothers' announcement.

Elias said, "People think we owe the Wilsons."

"We know we don't owe them nothing," Jude said.

"My good name is important," Rufus said. "I can't leave with people thinking I owe money. Maybe I should walk over and have a little talk with the Wilson brothers. Maybe they just don't understand."

"No!" "No!" "No!" A chorus of noes exploded as the family faced Rufus. "No, Daddy." Elias held his daddy down. "No."

Shortning saw terror and agony in his mama's eyes. His brothers and Peanuts had twisted expressions and hands over their mouths.

Lord! If Daddy did something like that, he would disappear quicker than lightning in a thunderstorm. It would be worse than when he tried to register to vote and the Klan beat him up and left him for dead. It would be like crawling in a den to have a friendly chat with rattlesnakes set to strike.

"I believe in the truth," Rufus said.

Shortning felt his face grow warm. Truth was, he had freed his daddy with a little made-up story. A rumor. A lie!

Hawk had told him the chain gang released Rufus Jackson because they heard the FBI was involved. When Hawk's father drove up and said he was from Sleepy Corners, the crew man said, "You come for Rufus Jackson? Take him. As far as we concerned, he ain't been here for two years, you hear? We ain't never seen him."

That's how his daddy was freed. Shortning felt confused and guilty, more than a little guilty. He knew his daddy was honest when he tried to solve their problems with head-on truth. But Shortning felt he was honest in another way when he tried to solve their problems around the truth.

He had no reason to feel guilty, he told himself. Faced with Mississippi meanness, he just had to do it this way sometimes.

Didn't birds like pheasant and grouse pretend to have a broken wing to draw a boy away from their ground nests? Weren't there moths with eyespotted little faces on their wings? Little faces that tricked the owls and other animals that might eat them? A katydid looked just like a green leaf, and walkingstick insects looked like brown twigs. And he and Peanuts had seen the wood duck pretend to be wounded to save its nestlings. For survival, nature was tricky too.

Yet, Shortning wished he didn't have to go around tricking his way through life. Would Chicago be different? He was wondering as his mama spoke.

"Our friends know we don't owe," she said.

"Daddy," James said, "we got to go north. You said."

"We know we don't owe them money," Rufus said. "Fact is they owe us big money this year. But the Wilsons say we owe. People think we do." Shortning felt confused again.

Some people borrowed money and bought on credit from the Wilsons' plantation store. The Jacksons didn't. The plantation store welcomed them, but they went to the general store. Only their cabin rent and farming expenses were subtracted from their pay. They should have big money coming at the November settle. It was all in a book, but the trouble was, the Wilsons kept the book!

Friday evening was clear and pretty for Miss Maybelle Clark's wedding. A band started playing at four o'clock on the sheriff's lawn. Shortning heard it from the cotton field. The wedding was for six o'clock.

No colored people were allowed to loiter nearby, so Shortning would have to hear about the wedding from the colored people who would serve food. But already he knew that Miss Maybelle didn't really have fifteen bridesmaids. That was a rumor. She only had twelve, and one of them was her sister. That meant that hers was not the biggest wedding in Sleepy Corners. But it was the only wedding where a father painted his house to match the bridesmaids' dresses!

Shortning went to bed earlier than usual on Friday. The family continued the arguments about whether or not they owed money. It seemed his daddy would never leave for Chicago, so again someone had to do something.

Saturday, in the dark of morning, squatting outside the cabin, Shortning and his brothers planned for leaving. They made the decision. Today was the last day. Miss Maybelle Clark's wedding was over, and they were no longer safe.

Shortning told Peanuts to meet him after milk delivery. High in an oak he waited for her. Finally he saw her.

"Quick," he said, climbing from the tree. "To church. Elias, Jude, and James agree. This is the day for action. We taking Daddy and Mama and leaving for Chicago today, whether Daddy's ready or not."

Together they hurried to the back door of the Mt. Olivet AME Church, which the men and women of the community had built. A small frame building, it was whitewashed outside and there were six windows on each side. On one windowsill rested a handbell that called the members to church on Sunday. Shortning knocked on the back door, and Miss Sadie opened it.

She hugged them. "At last. So glad to see you here."

"Miss Sadie," Shortning said, "we need the charity box."

Sadie opened a space under the raised pulpit and dragged out several cardboard boxes. "Here, you help yourselves," she said. She returned to work at a desk.

"Quick," said Shortning, "pick a dress too big for Mama. A fat lady dress. And a dress for you. Short. Not red."

He tore through the men's clothing, searching frantically.

Peanuts said, "We ain't got no money to pay."

Sadie called, "Won't cost you nothing. Do like your brother say, and quick. I got newspaper to wrap around what you take."

Shortning held a man's tan suit up. He measured the pants legs against his side, nodded, and chose more pants and some shirts. He searched among a dozen men's shoes. He tried on one pair. Then he chose some shoes, and Sunday straw hats.

"We can't take all this," Peanuts whispered.

Shortning said, "You want Daddy to live, don't you? Then help me. Help me find a shirt for Elias's broad shoulders."

All week he had felt like a rubber band stretched to break, but he felt better now that he was doing something. Convincing Daddy would be a hard job though.

"Peanuts," he said, "you'll have to sweet-talk Daddy into going, you know."

But Daddy knew, he thought. He was the one who had first said they had to leave. Now that the sheriff's daughter was married, nothing was stopping Sheriff Titus Clark. Everyone knew that. He was piling up shoes.

"All those shoes?"

Sadie called over her shoulder. "Take them all. Wrap them up. He's right, Peanuts."

Shortning pointed. "Head scarves for three."

"We don't wear no head scarves like slaves. We wear hats."

"Three head scarves, one for you and one for Mama and one for James. He's small," Shortning said. "And a dress for James that's long enough to cover his lumpy legs."

Peanuts giggled. "Shortning Bread Jackson," she said, "you sure are some tricky!"

Shortning winced. That was a compliment, but not the kind he liked. What a way to live!

He helped Peanuts carry the clothes bundles to their cabin; then he took off alone. It was still early and he had someone to visit. He hoped it wouldn't get him into trouble.

FIFTEEN

BACK IN SLEEPY CORNERS, Shortning broke off a branch of live oak. He passed the post office home of the Bakers three times before the postal service room was empty. It was about ten o'clock Saturday now.

He placed the branch on the steps, pointing up the lane, knocked, and walked away whistling.

In ten minutes, carrying the twig, Hawk Baker wandered to the largest live oak up the lane from his house. He whistled. Shortning whistled back and leaned out of the tree. Hawk was pretty smart for a white boy, Shortning thought.

"Well, climb up," he said.

Hawk stared at the lowest branch. "I don't know how."

"Come on. I'll show you. Everybody got to know how to climb a tree."

A car rolled near. Hawk bent over and tied his shoes until the lane was clear.

"All right," Shortning said, "jump for that low branch."

Mouth open, Hawk raised his eyebrows when he caught it. Shortning braced himself and tugged at Hawk, who walked his feet against the tree trunk. His face was red as he reached a broad tree limb for sitting. Clutching the trunk and branch he sat on, he stared all around him.

Like sunrise, a smile spread slowly across his face. He sighed. "Hi," Hawk said.

"Hi."

"I been practicing with spoons. They keep dropping."

Shortning laughed. "I could show you how."

"Tell me," Hawk asked, "what does Mississippi chariot mean to colored people?"

Shortning looked away. "Nothing."

"It means something."

"Chariot from Mississippi, that's what."

"No," Hawk said. "Please. You can tell me. Pretend I ain't white."

"If you was colored, you'd know." But Shortning looked at Hawk. He had cousins as white as Hawk.

"Well," Hawk said, "the colored people are all whispering it about your family."

Eyes wide, Shortning Bread choked on spittle, coughed and coughed. He could hardly breathe for a minute or two.

In a hoarse voice, he said, "Chariot means trouble, trouble leading to death. Comes from the old slave hymn, 'Chariot Coming for to Carry Me Home.' Home to heaven."

"Oh. Does that mean your family ain't safe around here?"

Shortning stared through the dense green leaves. He picked graceful gray-green moss and ripped it to pieces. Did this white boy think he was telling Shortning something new? He blinked to make sure there weren't any tears in his eyes. Hawk was staring at him.

Everything was planned. Elias had chosen the best routes out of town. He and Peanuts had clothes to disguise the family. This was the last time he'd see Hawk, but he couldn't tell him that.

"Hey," Shortning said to change the subject, "is Hawk your nickname? What's your real name?"

"My daddy had a pet hawk once, so he called me Hawk.

But my real name is Andrew Jackson Baker after the famous general and U.S. president. He chased the Indians out of Mississippi." Hawk perched proudly on the shaky tree limb.

Across from him Shortning winced and looked away. White people treated both Indians and colored people badly.

Hawk cleared his throat. "Maybe that was mean too. Maybe they were just people." He looked down and his face grew red against white hair.

Shortning said nothing. Toad in the mud, he thought. White is white, and colored is colored. I can't be true friends with this white boy. He don't understand about life.

"Hey," Hawk said, looking down the lane. "There go my folks to pick up the mail. Come on up to the house. They'll be away for a while."

"Oh no," Shortning said, "I ain't going in your house. We Jacksons in enough trouble and you don't want your mama and daddy be called 'nigger lovers,' do you?"

Hawk jerked his head to stare at Shortning. He took a deep breath and let it out slowly.

"I heard my mama and daddy talking one night since your daddy was freed. They say Jim Crow treatment of coloreds is evil. They say they ain't never known no colored folks, but they might be the same as us. See"—and he raised his head proudly—"they won't mind you in the house."

Hawk began to swing down, shaky on the next branch. He fell, but he stood up smiling and brushing his knickers.

"I'll go in the front door and open the back for you. Just duck in when nobody's watching." His face reddened, but he shrugged. "After all, we live in Mississippi."

Shortning nodded yes, while his brain screeched no. He was used to going in the back door. He had never entered a white person's front door, but suddenly he wanted to.

Desperately he wanted to walk into Hawk's front door. Just once he wanted to show white folks in Mississippi that he knew he was as good as they were. Besides, Hawk's front door wasn't like a real front door; it was a citizens' postal service door.

For a moment he remembered his daddy trying to register to vote. He shoved the memory out of his mind. This was different.

Play with Hawk in his house? This was his last chance ever.

No, no, no rang in his skull like an empty pail hitting the sides of a stone well. You can be arrested for breaking in! Your family will never leave for Chicago if you get caught. Shortning leaned from the branch and tried to call no to Hawk. His throat wouldn't let the word out.

Play with Hawk in his house? Would it be fun? Did Hawk have toys? Could Shortning touch the piano?

Hawk turned in the dusty lane and smiled toward Shortning. He turned back and hurried past his mama's square rose garden to his front gate. Shortning began to climb down.

SHORTNING BREAD WALKED the dusty lane slowly. It was about 10:30 on Saturday now. Dust soothed the toes of his bare feet, but suddenly he felt something besides dust. Something hard and round. He stooped and picked up a penny. A feeling of dangerous arrogance surged over him. He owned a penny. In his hand he held a penny!

He could sense Hawk's eyes watching him from around the shades at the kitchen window. Hawk's mother lowered shades on the south side of the house. People did that to cool the house while the sun was high. At sunset, they opened their houses to cooler air.

Shortning watched people enter the post office. Some people had mail delivered to box numbers there. He passed the rear gate. The back door was open wide behind a screen door, and Hawk was waiting inside that screen door; but Shortning Bread Jackson had a penny. As he passed the side yard, he sniffed the rose fragrance, and wondered if Hawk's house smelled like roses.

He held his penny tight between his thumb and first finger, and walked past the front gate and on down the lane. I got a right, he told himself, but he was spurting perspiration. I own a penny, he thought. He bought from Hopkins's store, why not buy from the post office?

He adjusted his floppy hat lower on his forehead. His suspender strap flipped against the back of his leg. Hawk would think he was crazy; well, he was crazy.

Shortning walked back and up the front walk like a true citizen. He sniffed the rose scents, noticed butterflies visiting roses. He stood aside as a lady came out, and he walked into the post office.

It smelled nice, like glue and paper, like school in winter. He stood aside properly while a man took his mail. Hawk came out and stared at Shortning. Hawk didn't look angry, just surprised.

Shortning cleared his throat, but no voice came. His hand shook as he held out his penny. Hawk nodded, reached behind a counter, and gave Shortning a stiff postcard. He held onto Shortning's hand until the man left.

"Quick," he said, swinging up the counter and pulling Shortning into rooms behind the post office. He closed the door with a sigh.

Shortning heaved a sigh too. He had done it! "Hey," he said, "you gave me two postcards." He held them out.

"Keep them," said Hawk.

"No." Shortning handed one back. "I only paid for one. Where do you live?"

Hawk laughed. "Here."

"No," Shortning said, "if I write it . . ." He pointed to the address side of his postcard, the first postcard he had ever held.

"Oh, we're Route One, Box Four, Pine Lane." And Hawk picked a letter off the dining room sideboard to show Shortning. Shortning stared at the address, at the letter.

"I don't think our family ever got a letter."

"Never got a letter? No mail at all?" Hawk stared and scratched his neck. "Come to think of it, we never get letters for colored people, and we're the only post office for Sleepy Corners, Rock Hill, and Swiftdale. My daddy don't deliver out your way."

Shortning picked up a long yellow pencil that smelled of good cedar. "Can I use this?"

"Sure."

He stared at it. Turned it around in his hand. On the sideboard there were pens, ink, and pencils. In the Jacksons' cabin there was nothing to read and nothing to write on. Mama had always wanted to own a Bible. Hawk's house had paper with nothing written on it. More paper than Shortning's teacher had at school! Shortning wrote:

Mr. Hawk Baker
Route 1 Box 4 Pine Lane
Sleepy Corners, Mississippi

He used the letter Hawk showed him for the form, but his teacher at school had shown them too. Funny, Shortning thought, when she taught them, he hadn't thought he'd ever write a letter. The addressed postcard went in his back pocket.

Hawk pulled his arm. "Come see my bedroom."

Shortning had been in homes before, washing windows, painting walls. But it had never occurred to him that a boy could have his own room. That a boy could have a bed, raised off the floor, all to himself.

He opened and shut his mouth. Hawk's room was just for him, and was larger than the Jacksons' cabin for seven people. Shortning could only stare.

Walls were papered in a design of tiny blue and red scrolls.

The room faced north, and pale blue curtains shook in a breeze through open windows with window screens.

On the floor in front of the bed, an oval rag rug lay like a shaggy dog. Pieces of thin wood, a penknife, glue, scissors, and parts of model airplanes covered a table across from the bed. Baseballs, a leather catcher's mitt, and two wooden bats stood guard in a corner. Looking up, Shortning saw airplanes, a half dozen of them in the air, hanging from string attached to the ceiling.

"Toad in the mud," he whispered, "is this your room for real?"

Hawk was enjoying his reaction. He shoved hands in pockets and rubbed a shoe on the floor. "Well, sometimes it's lonely," he said. "I don't have a sister named . . ."

Shortning smiled. So Hawk still didn't know Peanuts's name. "It's Caroline after my mama's mama."

"No," Hawk said. "That's not what they call her."

"Peanuts."

"That's it!"

Shortning reached and touched an airplane. A red rubber band hung by the propellers.

Hawk ran to his desk for another airplane. "Let me show you." He wound a rubber band to power the propeller, and released the airplane. It flew across the room and bumped the wall. Hawk laughed.

Shortning flinched. He'd never make a fine toy like that hit a wall. Didn't Hawk know it might break?

Hawk turned a knob on a big box made out of polished wood, with a gilded cloth over a hole. A radio crackled on, playing music. Shortning stared. All his life he had heard the radio at Hopkins's store, but he had never seen one.

Hawk sat and bounced on his bed. Three straight chairs sat against the wall, and an armchair sat in front of the table. A small bookcase was beside the table. Shortning sat cross-legged on the floor. How he wished Peanuts were there to see this!

"What's your favorite animal?" Hawk asked.

"You first."

"No, you first. I asked."

"Both together then," Shortning said laughing. "Wait, let me think. Now!"

"Toad!" "Bird!" they called.

"Why toad?" asked Hawk.

Shortning shrugged. "I don't know. I like them, that's all. They little and squat and funny and keep cool in wet mud. Why birds?"

Hawk raised his arms. "They soar in the sky and are free, and besides, they're pretty. And they make music." He turned the music on the radio to play louder.

"Butterflies," Shortning said. "Are they animals? I love butterflies." He stood up, raised his arms, and fluttered around the room like a butterfly. Hawk stood, lifted his arms, and soared like a bird. They wound around each other making humming sounds.

Laughing, bumping each other's hips and shoulders, they began to run wildly around the room. Soon they were wrestling on the floor, boy over boy, rolling, laughing. Hawk was strong, but so was Shortning. He laughed; this was fun. The radio announcer was giving news at noon. They had played since 10:30. Shortning saw Hawk stare over Shortning's shoulder. Shortning snapped around.

Mr. and Mrs. Charlie Baker stood in the doorway. She was

wearing a purple-and-white flowered dress and hugged a small, flat purse. Mr. Charlie Baker had his postal shirt unbuttoned at the neck. They stared at Shortning as if he were a rattlesnake loose in the house.

S E V E N T E E N

🦅

PANTING, CHEST HEAVING, Shortning Bread leaped to his feet, picked up his hat, and held it across his chest. Hawk lay on the floor, gasping. To Shortning, Hawk's parents didn't look like people who approved of their play. Instead, they looked fearful, even terrified.

Mrs. Baker recovered sooner than her husband. She stumbled across the room and jerked the window shades down, then walked toward the radio. Shortning thought she would turn it lower because Hawk had the announcer speaking loudly. She turned it even louder. Then she looked at her husband.

Mr. Charlie Baker still hadn't closed his mouth. His face grew redder and redder, ears flaming.

Shortning felt sorry for them. He couldn't understand at first, but he understood when he heard the voice of the sheriff's wife.

"Charlie," piped a shrill voice, "you understand that Titus don't find no fault with your postal service. And we understand with that nigger boy saving your boy's life . . ."

Shortning looked at the windows. He could leap out, but the screens would be too difficult to unhook. He ducked past Mr. Charlie Baker and saw Mrs. Titus Clark in the post office. She didn't see him, but she could see directly through to the back door. He couldn't run out that way.

He slipped into a room across from Hawk's bedroom; he supposed it was a pantry. Dining room, pantry, and kitchen seemed to be on the south side of the hall, two bedrooms on the north. Wall shelves in the pantry held cans of food lined up neatly. A pump handle poked up from a low sink. Potatoes and onions were in baskets on a shelf, and the noisy refrigerator motor chugged by his ear.

Mrs. Titus Clark passed him and marched flat-footed into the kitchen. Plopping a huge white purse on the table, she sat in a chair that creaked. Shortning heard Mrs. Baker fill her teakettle and strike a match.

He stared around. People were in the post office. The pantry had no door, so he couldn't hide there long, and yes, Sheriff Titus Clark was going to walk into the kitchen too.

Shortning backed against the wall and noisily bumped a galvanized pail. Trembling violently, he picked it up and began pumping water into the pail. A mop sat beside the pump.

The Clarks did most of the talking. Shortning heard Mr. Charlie Baker say, "I'm glad you understand how we felt about Hawk's life. He's our only child of twenty years' marriage."

"That nigger boy probably was trying to drown him, did you ever think of that?" asked the sheriff. He threw his hat on the kitchen table beside his wife's purse.

"Now that Maybelle's married off, we have to tend to business in Sleepy Corners."

Shortning tossed some powdered soap into the cold water, swished it with his hand, and pulled his hat down over his face. He felt someone unclip his brown suspender. He swung around.

Hawk held a finger to his lips as he began clipping a red

suspender to Shortning's pants, pulled a white short-sleeved shirt over Shortning's plaid one, then finished attaching the red suspenders. Shortning buttoned the shirt, tucked his old collar under the white collar, and tucked the big white shirt in his pants. He gave Hawk his brown suspenders. He had worn them until Daddy came home, and now he wanted his friend to have them. Hawk backed out of the pantry.

Shortning's admiration of Hawk increased. Maybe Hawk understood how things were, after all. Here was a boy with brains, even if he was white. Starting in the hall, Shortning began mopping; he used the wet mop first, then wiped the floor drier with a wrung-out mop. The floor was gritty from dust. He did a thorough mopping of the post office's black-and-white linoleum. Then he worked his way toward the kitchen.

Sheriff Clark said, "We can't let Rufus Jackson go scot-free after serving on the chain gang. You good people can understand that. What he tells young niggers could be dangerous to us here."

Toad in the mud! thought Shortning. The sheriff was starting another rumor! Another excuse for meanness.

The Bakers and Clarks moved aside as Shortning mopped the floor under their very feet. No one looked at him. The Bakers were silent, but Mrs. Baker dumped five pounds of flour in a huge pot. She worked cakes of yeast and warm water from the kettle into the flour. Hawk had disappeared somewhere. His radio was turned off now.

"You good folks don't have to do nothing," said Sheriff Clark. "That FBI man ain't coming back." He stood and twirled his sheriff hat. "Just don't get in the way of those of us serving our white southern way of life. It's our duty, you understand?"

Titus Clark stood, feet placed far apart, long legs bending and straightening at the knees. When Mr. Charlie Baker stood, he was much shorter. The postmaster's face was no longer red; it was so blue-white that it looked the color of china plates in the hardware store. He didn't answer. Mrs. Baker's lips were set in a thin, pale line.

She kneaded the bread vigorously around and around in the pot. Shortning Bread's mama kneaded bread on the table. That was a lot of dough Mrs. Baker was punching and twirling. Shortning had a feeling about it.

The kitchen clock read one o'clock. He had to study Elias's routes, and get home to warn the family.

He dumped the dirty water by the roses as if he mopped floors for the Bakers every day. He left the wet mop standing against the back step, head up to dry. The pail he turned upside down to drain. He felt good fooling the sheriff. He had scrubbed floors with a mop before. Housecleaning and laundry were how his family stayed out of debt to the Wilson brothers.

He couldn't help thinking: At the settle in November, they always cleared planting and tool debts, and they usually made money. They were healthy and strong, thanks to the Lord, as his mama would say. Still, getting ahead was difficult when they tried to keep James and Shortning and Peanuts in school. As Shortning thought of how hard his family worked, tears stung his eyes.

He had to stop thinking about the settle and the Wilson brothers. It could make him lose his mind, go crazy!

He closed the back gate and turned up the lane at an easy, loping walk. He was walking away from his home, but other colored people lived on other cotton fields. As soon as he passed a couple of lanes, he entered a woodland patch. A pine cone fell at his feet. He looked up. Peanuts perched in a tree like a redbird. He scrambled up.

"How come you're here?" he asked.

"I knew you'd come this way to fool them," she told him.

"The sheriff is after Daddy," he said. "We really, really got to leave today!"

She said, "I know. The Wilson brothers have men with guns guarding the sharecropper cabins. They say it's so nobody passes out Chicago job notices."

"Guns?" Shortning's heart seemed to stop. "That means our daddy's a target for killing tonight."

SHORTNING FOLDED THE WHITE shirt and red suspenders into a neat bundle. Then he and Peanuts set out walking, while he told her everything about Hawk's house. He was sorry he hadn't gotten to touch the piano and so was she. For an hour or so he and Peanuts carefully checked out the lanes heading north that Elias had told them about. They arrived home about three o'clock that Saturday afternoon. Elias was standing in the doorway.

"I hear you were in the Bakers' this morning with Sheriff Clark there," he said. "Where'd you hide?"

"Never you mind," Shortning told him. "Quick! We got to leave now!"

"No," his father said from behind Elias. "We leave at midnight. Mama's got cooking and laundry."

Shortning looked at Peanuts and nodded for her to talk to him. She knelt by their daddy and hugged him. "They expect us to leave in the night. Men guarding the fields will hunt us down. Shortning's right, Daddy. We got to leave now while it's daylight." She kissed his cheek. "Wait till you see what we got for you."

Shortning looked all around the cabin. He sucked in his breath. "They're gone."

"No, Brother," Peanuts said, grinning. "You looking everywhere but . . ."

He looked up. Balanced on a crossbeam were the newspaper bundles. He knocked them down with the broom handle and tore into the clothes. His hands were shaking like leaves in the wind.

Claudia climbed in the doorway with a bucket of water.

"Here, Mama," Shortning said, holding out a huge floppy dress. He ripped down the clothesline that held the sheet to divide the room, and cut the rope.

"Peanuts, get the thin mattress." He helped his startled mama wrap the mattress pad around her middle. He tied it with clothesline. The blue floppy dress covered their suddenly fat mama well. Next, Shortning handed out shoes.

Peanuts changed clothes and hung her red taffeta dress on the wall. She wore three dresses, a white one on top. "How we wrap these on our heads?" she asked her mama. She held out the head scarves.

Elias helped his father into the new shirt and suit pants. The tan suit jacket hung loosely. They were all sweating from a case of Mississippi afternoon heat and Mississippi danger nerves. Elias explained about the best routes leading north.

Claudia said, "My dishes ain't washed. The stove's ready for cooking. Laundry's on the line."

"Right, Mama," Peanuts said. "Nobody expects you to leave beans cooking and clothes for Mrs. Clara Davis on the line."

Claudia started to undress from her traveling outfit. Peanuts stopped her. "But, Mama, that's why we'll have to go now! We'll make it too!"

Claudia looked around her helplessly. She wrung her hands.

Rufus muttered, "People think we owe the Wilson brothers."

Claudia put hands on hips. "God almighty! It ain't what people think, Rufus, it's what the Lord knows!" She wrung her hands again. "The children are right. But we don't have no dinner, no grits, no bread," she said sadly. "I should've cooked . . ."

"I'll get food on the way, Mama," Shortning said. "We'll meet at the patch of live oaks north of Swiftdale County. I'll have food." He remembered that bread dough, an unspoken message.

Quickly his father turned. "Shortning, we don't steal. Before we steal, we starve."

"Daddy," Shortning said, "don't you worry none." But he didn't agree with his daddy. He'd beg or trick people. Maybe if they were starving, he'd even steal. There was always a way around a problem. They had a right to live; he and Peanuts knew that.

A surprised James called, "Dress like a woman? Never me!"

"You got to," Shortning said. "You guarding our fat mama. She need you."

"You crazy. You twelve years old and bossing everybody around," said James. He pulled on the dress anyway, and wrapped a head scarf into a turban. He and Claudia left first, two 'women' with laundry baskets going into Sleepy Corners.

Peanuts pulled her dressed-up daddy over the doorsill.

Shortning told her, "Take him through the fields first, and leave from other cabins. You know the best lanes."

Her eyes were tearful. Shortning took her hand as she stood on the top ladder rung. "Daddy need you."

Peanuts turned and took her father by the hand. With his Sunday straw hat and tan suit, he looked like a preacher, not a sharecropper. Looking back, he stumbled away, led by Peanuts.

Watching them leave, Shortning blinked tears. He looked around. "Where's Jude?" he asked Elias, who was dressing.

Elias fit into the pants, but the shirt was tight across his shoulders. Shortning had been afraid of that. He handed him a huge black jacket and a yellow straw hat with a hole in the crease.

Elias pointed. Jude and Annie Louise came up the ladder and stared around. They were dressed up.

"Where you been?" asked Elias, folding his arms. "We're leaving now."

"The preacher just married us," Jude said, grinning. "My wife's going with us. Where's everybody?"

"Gone," Elias said. "You two head out. We're meeting north of Swiftdale County in that patch of live oaks."

Shortning bound up extra clothes and a mattress, wrapped it with the last of the clothesline, and gave it to Annie Lou. She smiled and took off her Sunday hat. After she put the hat under the clothesline, she lifted the bundle onto her head.

Shortning knew she understood. A colored woman with a clothes bundle was all right. Elias told them the best lanes leading north. Jude walked away with Annie Louise, his new wife.

Shortning dressed in new long pants, Hawk's shirt and red suspenders, and a pair of shoes too long for his feet.

Hat on, Elias stepped out the door and stood on the ladder. "I'll watch to see that you don't get caught," he said.

"I'm all right, I'm a boy," Shortning said. "You're a man, you're in more danger. I'll put water with the white beans so they won't burn for a while. Go on now."

Elias stood on the ladder. "You sure?"

Shortning knew he had left something. He patted the pocket of his old pants that were hanging on the wall and took out the postcard. Now he was almost ready, but not quite. Elias stood watching.

"Go on," Shortning said. "Quick."

Elias lingered for a second, then jumped down and faded into the distance. The afternoon sun flared lavender red and lit the sharecroppers' cabins into gentle gold.

Holding his forehead, Shortning stared around him. Everyone had left so quickly. It was barely an hour since he and Peanuts had walked in at three o'clock. So fast, and they had forgotten something; what was it?

Also, he wanted to give something to Hawk Baker; but what did he have?

N I N E T E E N

꩜

*H*AWK HAD AIRPLANE models, and a catcher's mitt, and baseballs, and even empty notebooks for writing whenever he wanted to. What could Shortning Bread Jackson give a boy like Hawk Baker?

Shortning gazed out the doorway. Elias was far gone. Good. He added water to the white beans and stirred them. An unfamiliar shadow filled the doorway beside him, and Shortning began singing loudly. Maybe the person would go away, he hoped. He sniffed the white beans. They had cooked for hours, and they smelled good.

> *"Mammy's little baby love shortnin', shortnin',*
> *Mammy's little baby love shortnin' bread.*
> *Put on the skillet, put on the lead,*
> *Mammy's goin' to make a little shortnin' bread.*
> *That ain't all she's goin' to do,*
> *Mammy's goin' to make a little coffee, too."*

"Where's Rufus Jackson?" a voice barked.

Shortning jumped. He saw a man dressed as a sheriff's deputy. So Sheriff Titus Clark wouldn't come up himself. He deputized Mr. O'Brian, who owned the hardware store.

Shortning stared at the man, took a deep breath, and held

it. What could he say? He heard his mama's voice saying, "I sought the Lord, and he answered me. From all my terrors, he set me free." He could pray.

He heard his daddy say, "Men got to be strong. Things bound to get better one day." His daddy was a dreamer, and so was he. This was the day things would get better. They were headed north. They would walk all the way to Chicago, if necessary.

The money in the lard can, that's what they had forgotten!

His thoughts were swirling, and he was still staring at Mr. O'Brian. What could he say? No answer was an answer too. He shuffled his feet and scratched his head.

A voice behind Mr. O'Brian asked, "Is he in there hiding?"

"No," said Mr. O'Brian. "There's only a stupid boy in here cooking beans. I can see the whole cabin. Just a boy."

"Is he wearing broken brown suspenders and a plaid shirt?"

"No," said Mr. O'Brian. "This ain't Rufus Jackson's boy." He backed down the ladder, and it creaked under his weight.

Shortning sang the next verse even louder.

"Three little fellows lying in bed,
Two was sick, and the other 'most dead.
Sent for the doctor, the doctor said,
'Feed them chilluns on shortnin' bread,'
Oh,
Mammy's little baby love shortnin', shortnin' . . ."

Shortning glanced out the door. Mr. O'Brian and the sheriff were looking in another cabin. Two men carrying guns stood by that ladder.

Shortning ran for the lard can and dumped the money in a rag. He tied the rag in a knot, and hung it securely on his red suspenders. No one stole from a rag. He picked up a flat-brim straw hat, but he touched his old felt hat tenderly. Yes.

He folded his old hat and tucked it in his pants.

For Hawk's present, he picked up one of their tin cups. Hawk had drunk from a tin cup when he visited. Cup in shirt and straw hat held to chest, he climbed down the ladder. Neighbors were pointing to a cabin down the way.

"I think Rufus live there," he heard a neighbor say. The neighbor stood by the field pump with the sheriff and the men with guns.

Shortning walked up to the pump and splashed his face and hands. He drank from it. All four armed men stared at him. He wondered if the sheriff would remember him from the Bakers' house that morning? Mopping the floor. Same shirt and red suspenders? No, the sheriff wasn't saying anything.

His neighbors standing by the pump would have been pale if they hadn't been so dark brown. He sensed them silently screaming, Get away from here, Shortning Bread Jackson! And he would, in due time. But first he'd hang around.

He wandered to visit some friends, played hide-and-go-seek for about five minutes. Out of the corner of his eye he saw someone by their cabin. He ran to hide by a post and look. What a surprise!

Miss Sadie was taking down the Davises' laundry. What would she do with it? Iron it? Return it clean but wrinkled? She wouldn't let Mrs. Clara Davis say Claudia Jackson stole her laundry. Wasn't that kind? Wouldn't Mama be pleased?

All the unspoken understanding and kindness among their friends and neighbors astonished Shortning. Everyone had seen them leave, but nobody knew about it when asked.

Now he really was ready to escape, if he could.

T W E N T Y

🪶

SHORTNING STROLLED THROUGH the field of cotton, careful to sing boldly and off-key, instead of whistling a tune as usual. When he reached the end of the cotton fields, he saw a dozen of the Wilson brothers' men spread out in a line, walking toward him with shotguns over their arms. One man lugged a coil of rope.

Rope meant a lynching. They were aiming to hang someone from a tree, and that someone was probably his daddy. He was walking straight for them, but they hadn't seen him yet. How could he hide in white shirt and red suspenders?

He rubbed his hair until it looked wild, he hoped. Then he began to limp and mutter: "Ain't got no chicken. I said, ain't got no chicken. No chicken, no pig. Eat a butterfly. Ain't got no . . ."

He shook his head. Over and over he repeated the words: "No chicken, no pig. Eat a butterfly. Ain't got . . ." Straight through the line of men he limped, muttering.

"Hey, you!" a man called.

Shaking his head, Shortning hobbled on, muttering.

"He's crazy," said one of the men. "Leave him alone. I think I know him."

Shortning frowned and looked at the rich black Delta dirt. Some colored people went crazy drinking rotgut liquor to escape a hard life; some went crazy from daily sharecropping for a mean landowner; some went crazy from being cheated every year at the settle. He knew people like that, and those men did too.

Shortning limped straight on. Although he was obviously leaving Wilson property, he must have fooled them into thinking he was not someone to be stopped. About five o'clock he reached Sleepy Corners safely.

On Pine Lane, Shortning walked toward the big live oak up the lane from the post office where Hawk Baker lived. Above him in the tree he saw a flour sack hanging high. Somehow he had expected that, and he smiled. He climbed up. He could smell the yeast bread before he reached it. More unspoken understanding and kindness. Inside there were loaves of bread, packed tightly and still warm.

Shortning reached into his shirt and took out the tin cup. He stuck the cup handle onto an oak twig, and covered the cup with his floppy tan felt hat. His hand trembled as he touched his hat one last time. With a sigh, he climbed down with the sack of bread. He stepped over the ditch and onto the lane with the sack over his shoulder just for a second, just so Hawk could see him.

Down the lane Hawk Baker had been tossing a ball in the air and catching it over and over. Shortning knew Hawk had been waiting for him, and he watched Hawk stop and run in his kitchen door. Shortning had just jumped the ditch to stroll into the safer woodland, when he heard piano music from Hawk's house.

Hawk played a medley: parts of Scott Joplin's "Maple Leaf Rag," and parts of Fats Waller's "Honeysuckle Rose." Shortning smiled, but his eyes brimmed with tears.

Hawk understood why he was leaving; and they would always be special friends. Born on the very same day, they didn't have to play together daily. They couldn't. Hawk had realized: "We live in Mississippi." But in spite of that, Hawk and Shortning had discovered each other, and could be true friends. He patted the postcard in his back pocket.

In the woods, pale green moths—moths and butterflies meant winged happiness to Shortning—fluttered ahead of him. The moths darted toward red trumpet flowers whose fragrance beckoned in the late afternoon.

Shortning felt the warm, good-smelling bread from Hawk's mama on his back; he thought of his daddy being brought back when Mr. Charlie Baker went to the chain gang officials. Brought back just before they wanted to kill him for telling the truth to the railroad investigators. He thought about finding that penny, walking in a front door, and the fun playing with Hawk. He remembered Miss Sadie giving them clothes at the church, and Miss Sadie taking down the Davises' laundry. He remembered their neighbors pointing to faraway cabins to fool the sheriff. All memories of Mississippi kindness!

Tears washed his face, but his heart was singing. His path was lit by a golden Mississippi sun in the west as he walked to meet his family.

BIBLIOGRAPHY

Grun, Bernard. *The Timetables of History*. New York: Simon & Schuster, 1979.

Lemann, Nicholas. *The Promised Land: The Great Black Migration and How It Changed America*. New York: Alfred A. Knopf, 1991.

Mirkin, Stanford M. *What Happened When*. New York: Ives Washburn, 1966.

Skates, John Ray. *Mississippi: A Bicentennial History*. New York: W. W. Norton, 1979.

Welty, Eudora. *One Time One Place: Mississippi in the Depression, a Snapshot Album*. New York: Random House, 1971.